Near Morning

For my cousin Sandra Lipps
and whose two sisters are
in this picture. I hope
you like these pieces
especially about ~~the~~
my ~~brother~~.

April 26, 1996
in Winnipeg

Near Morning

By Robert Hilles

Black Moss Press

© Copyright Robert Hilles 1995
Published by Black Moss Press 2450 Byng Road
Windsor, Ontario N8W 3E8
Black Moss books are published with the assistance of the
Canada Council, the Ontario Arts Council and
the Department of Canadian Heritage.

Black Moss books are distributed by Firefly Books,
250 Sparks Ave., Willowdale, Ontario M2H 2S4.
All orders should be directed there.

Cover photograph by Paul Quenon. Cover design by Richard Withey.

Canadian Cataloguing in Publication Data:
Hilles, Robert, 1951—
Short stories.
ISBN 0-88753-271-3

1. Title.
PS8565.I48N43 1995   C813' .54   C95-900508-0
PR9199.3H483N43 1995

Many of these pieces have appeared or will appear in various publications. I wish to thank the editors of those publications for their editorial
suggestions and faith: Event, Grain, Writ, Secrets From the Orange
Couch, Canadian Fiction Magazine and in the anthologies Snapshots:
The New Canadian Fiction, Boundless Alberta, and Our Fathers

I would also like to acknowledge and thank the Alberta Foundation for
the Arts for its financial support during the writing of this book.

Table of Contents

Our Fathers

Looking At Horses

Quiet Nights

For the two Austins:
Austin Carey Hilles my son
and
Austin Edwin Hilles my father
For Rebecca with thanks for her editorial assistance.

And again for Breanne

with a special thanks to Marty Gervais for all his support and
Betsy Struthers for her careful editing

Our Fathers

Ares

My father died before I was born. His last breath expired in the bed where I was born. My mother was my father all of my life. She would show me how he walked and talked and I could only see her there. She had such tender small eyes but when she played my father she stretched them so they looked hard and precise. Her mouth when it wore his words was cruel and large. She loved my father until she died. She said his name with her last breaths. By then her hands were frail and yet she lifted one to my shoulder and smiled as if my father were standing just behind me.

She never had a picture of him except what she carried in her mind. But she never wavered in her vision of him. I don't know if I would have loved my father or even liked him. I am not my mother and can't say that I love men the same way she did. Sometimes my father speaks to me but it is always with my mother's voice. He never says anything about love just how he misses the shine in my eyes although he has never seen them. I have a son of my own now and he walks the way I know my father did. I'm not sure if I like that, though I've never done anything about it. I know my father was rough and callous even though my mother never told me that. I could tell by the way she changed when she talked about him. It was the roughness that took his life. When my son is rough I tell him to be gentle but he soon forgets and is rough again with the cat or one of his friends. But he is never rough to me, just holds me so tight before he goes to bed.

I never visit my father's grave although I visit my mother's often. When I am there with my son he says: "Grandma can you hear me? Grandma can I visit you for awhile. I've never been in heaven before." Later he asks me if grandma can hear him and I answer yes even though I am not sure myself. At night when my son is asleep I sit and think about the lessons that mothers and fathers pass on. And sometimes I wish that my father had lived so I would know for sure the power he had in his hands. But I know only what my mother has shown me and that is not how one should find their father. I would like to know for sure if he was cruel, since I find it hard to understand why sometimes I am cruel. Perhaps he could have shown me where cruelty comes from or how it can be stopped.

Apollo

On his deathbed, he remembered being a teenager and what it was like to have a god for a father, someone who could change your thoughts while you slept. There had been ideas he'd had as a teenager, ideas that now seemed silly but then they were powerful and new, coming from a part of himself his father didn't know. They were wild ideas. His father wasn't a bad father, just didn't know how to deal with a son who had ideas of his own. One night he was visited by the Muses and they left magical notes on his lips. In the morning when he spoke he spoke music. His father went to his side and kissed his hands as if he knew that his son was saved at last. But the son ran out of the house into the street as if he were pursued by an angel of fire. The boy never sang to his father or ever allowed him to come near him again. Yet everywhere he went, the music followed him and made him feel a captive of his own gift. Now near death he can feel the music finally leave him and he wishes his father was here so that he could speak to him and kiss him. Turning away from life and toward death like a sleeper turns from one side to the other, he sees his father standing in the distance with outstretched hands singing in his soft voice all his son's notes.

Hermes

He steals from the dead and the dying. But I love him and take his gifts without question. Some nights before I go to sleep he tells me stories about his crimes and I like that. He reveals his dreams too the ones he wakes in wearing a goat's head. Or where the earth and sky are pressing into his chest.

Most mornings he wakes me by dangling something he has stolen the night before in my face. I take it and embrace him and call what is wild, out into the light. He used to sell cars before he met me. He has never owned a new car or even a new suit. When he sleeps he hears the dying coming for him but they always stop outside the bedroom. He doesn't want to be old or to ever enter an embrace with death. I learned from him that a lover steals for his beloved first and for himself second. He has small quick hands that could take your life if necessary.

He doesn't want much from me except to love how his fingers can find me in the middle of the night opening my body in ways I find hard to refuse. Some nights I can hear him coming back in with his bounty. I can feel him collapse into a chair waiting for hours before coming to my arms as I hold his sleep for him. I like it when his sighs fill my sleep. When I am sick he doesn't go out but stays to wipe down my forehead and tell me a story. Once he told me of the day he stole a jewel from his mother's room and for weeks after he slept with it under his pillow. She must have known it was there but never tried to claim it or confront him with it. Each night it pressed into his flesh making his sleep a little more difficult. Finally when he could not sleep at all he returned it. Once he had returned it he knew he could steal.

I can't separate the truth from his stories. He always says a thief doesn't deal in truth and I guess he's right. I like the smell of him when I wake and he smiles at me, reaching for me tenderly. Some days I look at him and how thin he is and I wonder where he gets the strength to do what he does. When he is old I will have to carry him to a dark place to die. I don't fear death. I can already hear the dead speak to me when I am alone and I like that. But I fear his death and wonder what he is trying to tell with his life, if anything. I look at his clothes when he is gone and imagine him standing in them holding out his arms as if he was supporting the world. I might take the arm of one of his shirts and smell him in it. I like the traces like that he leaves on things not so much for me to find but just to let others know his crimes are not all he is. Often he takes my hand when I am about to go out somewhere and just looks at me for a moment as if my body alone were telling him all he needed to know. Then he lets go without saying anything his fingers squeezing the air where my hand just was.

Hades

Each day he returned home covered in coal. I don't know if he liked it underground we never talked about that. Every morning he would wake me with his coughing as he got ready for work. I would watch him from my bed as he sat at the table drinking his tea and looking straight in front of him as if his father was seated across from him. Sometimes he would speak quietly to his tea or hum a little when he couldn't find the words. I would turn over and listen to him with my eyes closed and I knew that a father was a sound in the morning someone who worked underground trying to find secrets there that he could bring home. His teeth were bad and they got worse each year and when he smiled nothing shone back from inside his mouth even his tongue was starting to turn black. And he would cough at night in his sleep as if he were answering back the gods that he found underground. Sad, stooping gods who could not tell you anything about the world because they had been below too long. Gods he would carry home in his lunch box and talk to them as if they were children that knew nothing of the world they inherited. He would tell me stories from the underground of boys who died in cave-ins before they had learned to use a razor. Once he was trapped for hours by a cave-in. He sang to himself to keep his spirits up. He never thought of death only of what the sun felt like on an arm in the early afternoon. When they found him, he was covered head to toe in an inch of coal dust only his eyes and mouth visible in the darkness. One of his legs was crushed when he was yet a boy and he walked with a limp and stooped over most of the time even when standing out in the sun. He taught me how our hands can only make or change a small part of the world, that underground people don't change just remember the outside better than most.

Near Morning

Some coal miners find their way out not with their lights but by following the draft from the surface. Some even worked in the dark to save on battery power turning their lights on now and then to make sure that their work was true. My father had small hands and they were always black and even the food he ate was covered in coal dust and every few months he would have my mother cut his hair so that it was not in his way when he worked. I never asked him if he liked his job or if it was what he wanted. We have never shared our dreams or talked about what a father or son might only what a father and son can. To him work was underground a place so dark even your body was invisible to you. I never went below to find out what it was like too frightened that I might like it or that my father would become someone else down there. When I was old enough to work in the mine, I left town to go to school and never came back until he died. He was still young. His lungs were so full of coal dust there was nothing they could do to save him. The night before his funeral I paced the rooms of our small house trying to decide if I should go down the shaft just once. In a foolish way I thought that I might find him still alive down there happy in his underworld talking and laughing with his friends so happy that the sun and the rest of the world didn't matter anymore. But I knew all I would find there would be the darkness he fled into death. There would be nothing of his down there nothing but a faint chill dragged down from the surface. I couldn't face that or the images in my mind of him stooped over reaching into the darkness for another shovel full of coal, another inch towards his own end. I didn't cry at the funeral just watched him being lowered into the earth and being covered like he was each day. The earth drained his life slowly until now all we could offer it was this frail skeleton. It did nothing, remained silent as it has always done, taking its own sweet time to reveal its secrets. It must have spoken to him and

17

told him things he could not bring back to the surface. But he never spoke of it, never let anything out, took it with him back down this last time no longer able to fight his way to the surface again. I will always remember him as he came in the front door each day covered in black dust smiling and whistling knowing that for the next few hours he would be in the light. Even at night at least there were the stars overhead and now and then the moon looking so optimistic all by itself crossing the night sky like a promise from someone brave.

Hestia

The house he built burned to the ground when I was eight. For weeks after, he would stand before the ashes and weep softly to himself while I waited in the car. He never built another house but moved instead to town and took a job as a clerk.

Today my father is old and sits in my new car as I stand before the clearing where his house once stood. I want to ask him where my bedroom was but he won't budge from the car. Now and then I look back but he ignores my stare. On the way back to town he will say: "Why did you take me there? Your mother isn't there. Neither is the wind. Neither is the hole where I drowned and came back to you." My father is old and we don't speak anymore. At least not in the normal sense. When he speaks it's as if he was far away as if he were trying to direct me to the place where he is. Perhaps it is his own death he is reaching me from.

He has forgotten most things. Even Mother, who died so many years ago, is only a word now. No face — no body left. Once, a year ago, he looked at my son and said: "My wife had such blue eyes." But her eyes were brown, at least that's how I remember them. I said nothing but smiled and nodded my head. He liked that and went back to listening to the world as though it was a sound deep in his chest.

Sometimes I want to put my head to where he listens to hear his breath settle gently in his chest for an instant or more before he pushes it back out again. But he won't let me close to him except when I dress him each morning moving his thin legs so that I can pull his pants on. It's hard to imagine his frail hands holding a hammer or aiming a saw. But I do remember the summer he built his house. I was six and I sat on each log as he shaved off the bark.

19

So strong he looked and yet delicate as if his hands could fashion the smallest piece of wood into something beautiful. Mother helped too as they placed log after log onto the walls.

Most of the time, he looks out the window as if one of the cars that passes on our street might be coming for him. I can't sum up his life and I don't want to and he wouldn't want me too, although we never talk about such things. I never ask him questions anymore I just wait for him to say something, listening to his words coming from somewhere in the middle of his memories. His life ended a long time ago, ended, perhaps, when Mother died. That's when he started to forget things. That's when he moved in with us. That's when I started to dress him. This isn't his life anymore it's my life. He knows that and tries to hide in my house, to be as small as he can.

After the house burned things started to fall apart. First my mother's mind went. For years after she was in and out of hospitals. Psychotic incidents they called it. As if a name like that could make a family whole again. That we could grow around Mother talking to herself. Denying that Dad was her husband. He died in the fire she said or during the war. Some time ago when they were still in love and could see through the clouds in their lives.

Once when my mother was well I brought them to the city to show them my new apartment when I was going to university. They didn't like Winnipeg, to them it was too full of tragedies. Every day in the news there were fires or car accidents. Too much grief my mother said one day. And I felt strange because I had never noticed going about my life cluttered by the debris of other people's lives but not caring.

They never came back and I followed them back to Kenora where we are now. I feel old too watching my father sitting so still sometimes I am afraid to go near him. Sometimes he'll watch TV but not for long. He'll fall asleep in the middle of the show and moan as he sleeps as if trying to sing somewhere deep inside.

I remember the day Mother died. Father was still strong then. He sat by her bed for the whole day never moving or speaking just touching her head once in a while and humming. I remember his gentle sad humming. It was the same humming he did when he put me to bed when I was a girl. I'm not sure he was even aware he was humming his mind suddenly retreating into some distant thoughts. Once Mother opened her eyes and smiled at him and then closed them, never to open them again. I wonder if he remembers that now if he can see her before him when he stares or when he dreams?

On warm days I take him out into the yard and he watches my children. He never speaks to them just listens to their youth. What does he learn from them, I wonder, and they from him? Mostly to them he is furniture, someone who decorates the living room or TV room. The young and old so opposite and yet they occupy the same land move to the same music their hearts and minds starting and finishing the same way.

When I put him to bed at night I don't sing to him like I did to my sons when they were younger. I mostly sit beside him and listen for his sleep to come. Sometimes at night he will call out and I run to his room expecting to find him dead or awake but he remains lost in his sleep held there for a few hours more, trapped among the odd workings of his mind.

When I was younger I didn't want to think about my parents as old or dead. I wanted them to stay the same age to let me catch up to them. Now my frail father occupies my house like a memory that is hard to hold onto. He sits with his hands folded and I imagine them gripping a hammer, imagine him telling me the story of how he and mum met. How he was cutting wood for her father and how at night they would talk until it grew dark. But he never told me that story, she did, and I have never been sure if it was true or how she wanted it to be. I could never ask him, never wanted to find out if love began differently for him than her.

Some mornings his feet stiffen up and I have to put them back in place before I can dress him. I never know if it hurts him. He never lets on even his eyes don't give up any secrets. When my mother started to lose control and go wild, he became more in control trying to balance things even though it was impossible to do so. He tried so hard just as she tried so hard to become free not of him so much as of her own mind of the world she woke up in but didn't like. The day of the fire my mother was visiting a friend. Saved from the flames because my father forgot to buy butter the day before. She would tell that story over and over and after awhile I hated it not because it wasn't true but because a person's life should be saved for better reasons than that. My father liked that story and would laugh every time she told it to some-one, laughed as if for the first time something he had done took on cosmic significance. Someone else might have blamed her for the fire said that perhaps she left something on the stove but he never said a thing. I'm not even sure now if that thought ever crossed his mind although I always thought about that possibili-ty.

What if the madness had started earlier, not triggered by the fire but something else in her life? Perhaps that was something my father feared more than the fact that she might have started the fire. My father was never interested in blame never said a thing could be blamed on someone or something. They just happened just like the wind never wakes and asks itself where it was, it is simply here, a part of things, never to blame just fitting in as it can.

I never listen at night to the wind or wonder what it might be if it wasn't for us framing it within our lives taking the time to name it and the things it does. My father taught me when I was young to listen but not with my ears or with my mind but with my body with what it held inside, not a soul or sound, something deep and unnameable unowned by anything except where I am and who I am. My mother taught me that the world is wild and crazy that sometimes going mad is the only way to escape, the only way to find what it is that haunts you.

Artemis

My mother was always a virgin. She said god came to her one night and placed me inside her. Not because he loved her but because he wanted something of his body to grow outside him. For a long time she would not name me, only referred to me as SON. My father had no body I could recognize, no face except what you see when closing your eyes at night. Sometimes when I was young my body twitched with fear and I thought of my father as the warm water that fills a bath or the sky when not a cloud can enter it. My mother was not in love with god and could care less what he did with his time.

She told me little of the world before I was born. She wasn't afraid of her body, exactly, but for her it was a question, something that covered her in an inexact way. I never asked her about my father or even if she loved him. She wanted to be left alone to grow old without giving answers.

As I grew up, she hardly aged at all. But when I was a man she aged very quickly until it seemed death was only a day or two away and so it stayed for many years. At night she would talk to herself cursing something that had happened a long time ago. When she did name me she used a name that was hard to say. I often wondered if my father came to her at night or if he asked of me or looked in while I was sleeping. But she would not say. I was sure he was not handsome or strong but someone who could only return at night, who was afraid to look out well lit windows. When I was a boy, my mother would tell me stories before I went to bed, not stories about the past or made up stories, but stories about my future. The places I would live. The people I would meet and love.

Near Morning

Once-in-awhile I thought that my father spoke through my mother, that her words entered her mouth on the breath she took in. Her voice was like the smoke from a cigarette spreading slowly around the room. And I listened holding my sleep in, my mother like a new word I was learning to shape. Each day she would drag herself off to work holding a cigarette and her purse, the few things her life contained. When I was a small boy, I would fall asleep in her arms and wake in her arms as she carried me downstairs to the landlady who watched me.

Each night she smelled of work and men. She would rinse her hands and rub them with cream and then make supper while I watched. Most days I waited for my father to come to the door, waited for my mother to introduce him to me. The men that visited her never looked as though they could be my father. Usually they smelled like they carried a curse they wanted to leave on her. I would listen from my bed as they talked and I wanted to surprise them and run the man from her life for good. She had eyes that men wanted and I cried at night because I couldn't hold the door closed for her. As I grew older, I learned how a body changes without our understanding, and how what our bodies are remains unknown even into death. We walk inside them keeping the right things at bay and yet from day to day there is little more than words and touching. It is easy to forget who you are, to look at a mother or father and imagine that they hold the right secrets or can say how it is that things are assembled but they can't.

If my father came to visit, I never heard him. Most nights there was no sound except what the city does on its own at night as I would turn from side to side trying to imagine my father standing before my mother and taking something from himself and planting it inside her much like a child takes a rock and places it on a dresser for safekeeping. My father made no sounds had no

25

voice except for something he loved. My mother never actually touched him never felt his warmth pass across her face. She wanted not to be caressed or kissed but to be set free to have her body assume a responsibility of its own.

Before she died her eyes took on a glow they never had before. And quietly she described my father to me, not how he looked or what he wore but his manner how he sounded as he moved from place to place in her room. She explained how his form changed as he moved about. Next to him, she could feel sounds most bodies do not let out. She could not hold him but waited as he waited, not for night but for something to be let out for the denial to stop. Finally he spoke and his voice was rough and confused. She did not love him did not want any part of him was not particularly interested in what a god could do for her. But she remained because something inside persuaded her.

After telling me all that, she could speak no more and slowly faded into death. I turned and half expected to find my father standing behind me but there was nothing but the cold walls of the hospital room. I stood one last time in the doorway of her room and heard her say his name and then my name and at last I could hear how my name came out of his and then I turned away to find where my father was to bring him news to show him what grew from his body was nothing more than what his body discarded.

I wanted him to know that when my mother died what she carried with her was not what he had left for her but something of her own making. Death not weak and sad but powerful and true something belonging completely to her. I sat in the dark for awhile before going to sleep that night but I found nothing in the sky to watch. All I could feel was on the inside claiming something here and something there the kind of feeling that only comes at times like this when even in the dark with my eyes tightly closed I could not find her death. I was nothing but a shell that started inside her just as she began in her mother and from time to time the world outside made sense but often it was little more than an echo of what was inside of what was before and comes again. My mother, with her dead eyes closed, no longer imagines my father no longer struggles with her body. She is protected for the first time by what her body could never share with her.

Athene

I was a foundling. My mother raised me as though I were her own child although she never pretended to be my mother. I can remember when I was very young she told me that she had found me one morning outside her apartment building. I was wrapped in blankets and only a few hours old. She never knew if my real mother was someone in the building or someone passing who thought this spot was safe. She never married and raised me on her own moving from town to town when the jobs changed. I loved her in the ways a child loves a parent looking at them for their own share of the future. I thought often about my real mother and father, what they must have looked like and how in desperation my mother must have covered me in her best blankets leaving me where she knew someone would find me. It's hard to be angry at someone you have never met and yet most of my life I have carried that anger inside never letting it out just keeping it there to help move me forward. My mother who raised me told me often about the city where I was born. But I have never been there nor to the apartment building which I think of as my birthplace. I can see it in my mind what the stairs must look like and the halls. But I have no memories, for my mother moved away shortly after finding me. I can remember riding trains, lots of trains. Every time my mother moved she took the train. I can remember waking in her arms the fields outside covered in snow. She would sing softly to me. Her eyes would be closed and I would watch her mouth for awhile her red lips opening and closing to shape the lyrics. She would rub my head slowly as she sang. I felt protected knowing that I had been found. As I grew older my body sought my real mother and father more. I would look in the mirror and try to imagine what faces had helped to form mine what variations of noses, what lips, what eyes. My mother kept to herself so I never learned much about men. Nothing could stop me from growing towards them from wondering how a man interferes with your life how his hands make you part with certain promises. I imagine my father with my real mother the day I was born. Imagine his happy face as he held me towards the sunlight in the room. Other times I imagine that my mother is my real mother that she did not find me but wanted others to think that to protect herself. Women were not meant to be on their own with children no husbands no fathers to make things legitimate. But would she have lied to me too? Would she have forgotten my father so easily?

My childhood was normal. I went to school, had friends. I did all the things that a growing girl does. I would watch my friends with their fathers and I would wonder how it felt to be held by one or told "I Love You." I imagined my father as short and stout, and smelling of beer and cigarettes. He would sleep in on the weekends and take me skating in the winter keeping me from falling with his hand in mine. The father I imagined never acted or spoke the way my friends' fathers did.

It's hard to forgive people you have never met but as I grew older I forgave my mother and father. One night alone in bed when the wind was particularly wild I thought that I must forgive them since they will never know that I do. I felt I must so that somehow they would find their lives easier that way. In truth it was my life that was easier. So much of the world is fact and yet most of it is unknown and inside of us as we speak or feel what can't be shown or transmitted. As I grow older I imagine my parents old like my mother carrying with them memories of a child on the day she was born. Never forgetting the first few sounds she made. What was life like for them clinging to something so fragile so brief? Did they have second thoughts and return an hour too late to claim me? Did they have other children they held onto? Did they stay together? And as I wonder the answers aren't as important as the questions. Knowing isn't as important as believing that things are possible. Sometimes at night I watch the stars and recognize that the light coming from those distant places is much older than my life or the mysteries that form it. I feel the moonlight on my hand and I imagine my real mother's face reflecting a similar glow. But the light does not reveal more than what it touches. It can't show what's inside or what the words can't confirm either. A connection of things held in our heads but felt all over.

If I did find my parents now what would I say to them? What would I ask other than how I was born and how they came to leave me? Would I be strong enough to ask them what their lives were like without me? Would I be able to see it in their faces and eyes? But what is the point to wonder, to live with such questions in my mind. What I want is something simple, to hear my real mother's voice, to walk with her for a while, to find out what she is like, to kiss her on the cheek once and smell her. I have no pictures to compare the years to. I have no single impression of her smile to see how her eyes grow old from one picture to the next. No way to see my father part his hair on one side then the other to see on his face the same questions I have. But I manage. I have my mother and my own life now. I move on watching the sky and the streets the same as I always have done. I can't know the weights that others carry for me. All I know is what I bear now. My back, strong and hopeful, keeps me upright. My father and mother do not know me. Do not know the woman I have become slowly over the years. Soon I will have children of my own. I will tuck them in at night and sing them songs tell them stories. Each story will bear a little of my life in it. I will love them as a parent does in her own peculiar way. But what will matter to them will be the sounds their mother and father make in the house. And if they wake in the night I will go to them from a sleep they can't visit. And I will carry to them what my sleep has left for me. In their rooms I will know that I can protect them for awhile. Then slowly they too will look around and start to reach out in ways that are all their own.

Demeter

She was a farm girl. Her father raised barley and corn among other things. But she ran away from home when she was sixteen. She fell in love with a drifter or so she said. By the time she had me, my father was long gone. She never talked about him much or had any pictures. Mostly she thought of him as dead. Not because he deserved to be dead so much as because his love for her did nothing more than bring me into the world.

She always told me she wanted a daughter, a daughter just like me, although I often found it hard to believe. I know she didn't want one the way she got me. She never talks about being pregnant with me or if my father was around then at all. My curiosity often drives me to ask her questions about those things but she usually doesn't answer turning away in sadness or despair. Growing up I never saw my grandparent's farm. My mother often talked about growing up there, about the fields of barley so private she liked to lose herself in them. Lying in the middle of one surrounded by their high summer stocks, she would think about things. About her life, about her body and how it responded in ways her parents would not talk about.

She lived thirty miles from the nearest neighbour and had no friends her age. Even the children she knew in school lived too far away to visit. All summer she would lose herself in the fields of barley. Her father was strict. He required her to do a hard day's work on the farm. But she always found time to hide in the field, to listen to the wind as it rushed through the swaying barley like a fire. She would close her eyes and listen to her body form the world inside her. The wind nothing but a reminder that there was something outside, something unknown and distant claiming everything around her a moment at a time. She felt safe among the barley hidden from everyone.

When I was born she nearly gave me up for adoption. But something stopped her. It wasn't the way I smelled, not like anything else in her life, or how vulnerable I looked. It was something outside her life, outside my life that stopped her. It wasn't the face of my father or the guilt she had learned so many years at home. Perhaps it was something the barley fields had told her, something the earth opened up to let her see.

She moved to Calgary with me and took a job as a receptionist, determined to not let my father ruin her life. I remember staying with friends of my mother while she worked all day. Day-care was hard to find in those days. On weekends she would take me on long walks past houses she wanted to live in but never said anything about them. Sometimes we would stop in front of one and watch the owner cut the grass or work in a flower bed. She never spoke or asked them a question just watched as if she was waiting for something to happen.

My father never came to find me, never once contacted my mother, never once offered to help her out — not that she would have accepted. I have often thought of my father not as a person in my life but as a sound, the wind perhaps, or the city outside, a sound that is there but takes on no meaning other than as a distant companion to my life. I imagine the colour of his hair or what his voice would sound like not because I long to find out but because I want him to have some physical qualities to remember.

I am not like my mother I don't seek a field of barley to bury myself in. I like to mingle on crowded streets or crowded rooms.

I like to hear other's voices to know that each carries with it a kind of love that could be found if enough attention was paid. Sometimes I search inside for my father just like my mother must have for her father when she was alone in those fields of barley. But I find nothing inside only the places where a father could be but isn't.

Once my mother took me for a ride to see a field of barley. She took my hand and towed me out into the middle of one. There we lay down for an hour or so watching the sky and listening. What I heard first was my heart growing inside me. I listened for my mother's heart but all I heard was the rustle of the barley. I half expected my father to find us there to stand above us smiling down as if all at once he had found what was missing in his life. But we were alone there except for the odd bird that healed itself in our vision. I wanted to get up and run through the barley but my mother stopped me angry that I had missed what she was trying to show me. When I think back to that day, I see she revealed a vulnerability I had never seen before. But I didn't notice still consumed by what the world offered.

Finally we got up and headed back to the car not changed but grown apart somehow. My mother finding that it was not her daughter she had felt before alone among the barley but something else, something that had drawn her to my father, something that was still too far away to name.

Only once before I left home did my mother speak about my father. One day when I was fifteen and certain that I was in love she told me the story of my father:

"He was not a handsome man nor young. He was in between in age. He walked like someone who had had a hard life. One morning he crossed a field of barley to my father's house. At first, he never said his name just asked for a drink of water. His clothes were covered in dust and flecks of the grain. Your grandfather told him to come inside but he didn't reply right away. Just looked around him as if somewhere on the horizon he needed to find something. Then he followed father into the kitchen holding his hat in front of him like an offering.

"When he sat down he came down hard and I heard the wood in the chair crack. My father felt sorry for him and asked him to stay for awhile to help with the farm. If he had known then what would happen, he would have had second thoughts. I was intrigued by him. I was your age and I was learning that my body knew more than I did about things like love. At night around the supper table he told us stories about his life, sad stories and happy stories. He told each one with his slow steady voice. Sometimes he would look at me a certain way and smile. I'm sure my parents never noticed this at first. Once he came out into the field where I was hiding and lay down with me and listened too. That was when I knew that my body was going to win. We started to meet out in the field and once we made love softly and for a long time. The sky was a shade of blue I had never seen before.

"It was only that once that we made love. The next day he was gone. I was never sure if it was from shame or fear of my father. Later I found out I was pregnant. I told your grandmother but I never told my father. One day I just packed some things and left not wanting to tell him what I had done. I remember as I walked the road towards the highway seeing my father on his tractor way out in the field his head was down looking at the barley as the machine lumbered on. He never once looked up never once saw his daughter leaving his life, her body already forming a new life inside her."

My mother never stopped once when she was telling that story nor did she cry. Once she took my hand and kissed it. I wasn't sure if she told me that story as a warning or as a release. That night I could find my father inside me for the first time. When I looked in the mirror, I could see his face transposed on mine. My dreams were filled with images of him walking with my mother through the barley or standing beside me holding a hat. He never spoke to me in my dreams or to my mother. Just filled a space that had previously been empty. Once I found myself saying, "Father you will never know me, never know how your daughter tugs at the corners of your life, will never know how she has looked into the night because that was where her father should be." When I woke the next day, I wanted to go once more to the barley fields with my mother to lie with her as the world repaired itself without us. I wanted to feel my father there too not because I wanted to love him or could love him or must love him but because I wanted my mother to know it was not him that she sought but me. The prairie, for a little while, held her dreams.

But we never have gone back to that field and my mother is old and when I visit her she never talks about barley only about what it means to be old. Her hands mend certain things when they touch mine and I can't say if she is happy or even if I am. All I know is that my father has never been anything but the wind outside distant and unknown making certain that some things can't be told without mentioning him. But still it is my mother that matters never waiting for him just moving ahead certain that it was her body and not her that made the mistake that took what he offered, his own body craving for my life.

Hera

My mother was afraid of my father. She had three children and bore each successive child more reluctantly not because of their increased weight but because she feared what part of their father each carried. I being the oldest watched each new arrival with curiosity and hatred. She hid me from his rages and at night I often heard them quarrelling. Three sons my mother hid inside from him as long as possible. Three times he took each child into his arms as if to smother it but something good inside stopped him.

When I was old enough to understand, she told me to run away when I grew up. Not to wait for her or my brothers but to take to the highway and never come back. She told me stories about boys who had run away from home and became famous, rich and happy. Some nights she would cry out softly for someone to save her but I remained in my room locked in my fear.

His voice was so powerful it stopped the wind and sun. He tasted power in everything he did and everything I tasted was flavoured by him by the power he collected around him like a boast. He never played with me when I was growing up only looked in on me after I had gone to sleep as if only then did I take on life. It was my mother who taught me about love and how it comes from the coldest part of your body. She told me that a father is a strange creature that owns the house but never lives in it, who talks to himself in the dark and makes you listen. Who comes to bed not to hold you but to possess you. She showed me the places on her body where he struck her. Even if he died a thousand deaths he couldn't start her love over again.

When I buried him I was thirty and I stood on his grave not as a victor but as a tenant. I spoke with him through the micro-

37

phone of earth that covered him. His answers were the things that he set free such as the wind. I did not ask him to love me nor did I forgive him. I merely told him what the world was like without him in it. I told him how the sun looked caught in my mother's eyes for the first time. I wanted him to see what he left behind was beautiful.

That day I entered the world for the first time. I started to carry him inside me. He could feel the places where I loved him and where I hated him. He could feel my mother's hatred as it came with every word she spoke. As I walked around the rooms he once roamed he could feel the toxins he had left behind. He is not my hero and clings to me like a condemned man who no longer has a god.

I will gladly bring him to where he wants to go for he belongs to me now, is no longer capable of revenge. I want his love to boil. I want my mother to take his power for herself but she never will. Instead she watches the northern lights at night as if their music could cleanse her. Light from them makes her face cold and blue like the light from a fading soul.

I want to kiss her cheek so that my father might feel what little of her he has left for others. But she turns to me as if she knew and does not smile but kisses me passing the blue light to me.

I did not run away as she coaxed me. I stayed until my brothers too had grown. Even though I could have, I never beat my father or pushed his face to the ground as I had wanted to do as a boy. She would not let me because she wanted to protect me. I could not protect her the same way nor save her. Some nights I hear her calling out still and I want to go to her but I can't my bed so far away my father deep inside me, his words coming from my mouth. Instead I call out for her with his words. My body a graveyard for their love my life a room they build for me with their eyes. I wait now hoping that one day I will wake alone.

Aphrodite

He didn't move out all at once, my father, but in stages. First, he took a suitcase full of clothes. When he left that day, he wasn't sad but I could see in his face that he didn't want to go. He loved my mother very much but she no longer wanted him there. She didn't want to keep bumping into his things. It drove her crazy that even in this he was so slow and uncertain. I wasn't on her side but I wasn't on his either. At fifteen, I was on my side and I wasn't sure what that was. All I knew was it wasn't theirs. My father ran a gift shop in town and it was in the back of it that he found my mother with another man. He didn't do anything at first just stood there staring as if he was trying to discover what they were doing. My father was never particularly smart or strong. As a boy he had found ways to get by the bigger boys. But left on his own in adulthood he hadn't done so well. He was not someone anyone took to very quickly. Shy and gentle he was behind the counter of his store every morning at 8:30 sharp. He wasn't sure what to do with a daughter he'd wanted a boy so much that when I was born he couldn't stop himself from crying and he left my mother all alone in the hospital for three days before he came for her. That is when she started to know. He was more comfortable behind the counter than he was with her or me. I helped out in the store but never got any closer to him. When he moved out of the house he moved into the store. The small room in the back was where he slept and ate. Some mornings I would go and bang on the door to wake him up and I would be able to tell by how long it took him to answer that he had been crying and may have cried the whole night. But he never wanted me to know that. I'm not afraid of him but he frightens me the way the world is so tight for him. He never lets go never lets anything out. Eventually my mother got tired of his slow progress in moving out and got her brothers to move all his stuff into the back of the store. By then there was little room left for anything but himself squeezing in through all his possessions. We never talked. If we did it was about the store what was selling what wasn't who was buying what and why. He liked knowing those parts of people's lives. Knowing in a small way the secrets that others would not know. He kept them secret too never telling anyone except me. Some days now I feel more like his sister than his daughter although we are not that close in age. My mother never took up with the man my father found her with although he tried to get her to move in with him. I am not sure if it was because of inertia or because all the years with my father were enough to make her want to live alone.

She never talks about my father now goes into work at the local supermarket everyday where she works as a cashier. Happy to be working for my father's competition. The irony never escapes her or him although neither acknowledges it openly. She doesn't like my helping out at the store but we can use the money so she never says anything. She knows I would never move in with him, could never stand the crowded decrepitude of his back room. Sometimes I wonder what it must be like to be either of them. I imagine myself with my father's broad shoulders and stooped over back walking the streets of town like an animal in pursuit of his own scent. I wonder how it must feel to shave in front of the mirror moving the blades over the wrinkles. Or my mother walking with her sure gait still knowing that what the mirror reflects is attractive and young. Some times I watch her small hands with fascination as she waves them as she talks pointing out a window as if by accident. She sometimes takes my hand with one of her small ones and strokes it and looks into my face perhaps trying to discover herself inside me somewhere. Looking out I feel awkward as if my body wasn't me but a shell I woke up in one morning when I was twelve.

My father never took up with other women. When they come into the store he pretends to be even busier than usual. It's not because he is awkward or no longer interested but because right now love is something he won't let himself pursue. He acts as if death would be a safer place for him. He is the most happy when the store is closed after a busy day and he can huddle in his back room watching the TV and eating from a can. Sometimes I stay with him an hour or two and watch with him. He never says much just watches the screen as if he was expecting my mother to come on any minute and invite him home. But he never asks me about her never wonders out loud what she is doing. He can tell from me that she is still alive. Perhaps that is all that is keeping him alive too. On those nights of watching TV my mother never asks where I have been coming in so late for supper as if she knew and could not bear to hear me mention him. Sure I want them together but I don't have the energy to pursue that either. Instead I move between them like a small storm bringing to each evidence of their former lives. I live in my own life one where they are two landmarks that I can heed or ignore. Most of the time I move through pain they can't imagine or hear just as they must although they never say. We live together so close so apart from one another as distant and as unknown as the stars. Mere pale glimpses of light that are impossible to ignore but equally impossible to feel any heat from.

Sometimes at night I imagine my parents together in the other room. I imagine them having long conversations about me, who I will become, who I am most like, what I did today that was so wonderful or so bad. Conversations I imagine they must have had when I was little as most parents do when things are awkward between them and they need something safe to talk about. It is something I crave now but between them there is only silence and distance and that is what I have become, something unspeakable to them. If I have children, I want them to know that my love for them is not held in the space that exists between parents but comes from inside me not ending at my mouth or eyes but moving out into the room like a warm breath after making love. As I try to fall asleep most nights, I try hard not to dream about them wanting so much to wake up having passed the night in my own world. I know that is impossible so instead I try to forget upon waking. And moving over the cold streets to my father's store, I know I carry my mother's scent and the scent of our house with me and my father must like that as I bring it with me into his small back room. Just as he imagines I carry his scent back to her hoping she will remember something that once was between them. But most days she is not home when I get there and his scent is lost on the furniture. Coming in after work, she looks so tired that love is the last thing on her mind. Sometimes we eat together other times one of us has already eaten by the time the other gets home. When we do eat together I imagine my father in one of the empty chairs at the table. Sometimes I see my mother watching me as I look at the chair. She probably knows what I'm thinking but says nothing just goes on eating as if love was a season that has passed.

The Fates

My mother was alone the day I was born. My father out in the fields all day did not see her signal. Our farm is a small one by most standards but it is still quite a distance out to where my father was working that day. He had taken a lunch so that my mother would not have to bring him one in her condition. When he got home that night my mother had a son to show him. He held me for a time and said my name, Lawrence, in a way that my mother has remembered ever since. He is not a big man but is very strong. His face plain and reserved. At night he and my mother hardly speak. He fills his plate with food and finishes it with a solemn command. I have seen my father near death many times but he has always pulled through. Going back to the fields as if his labour is what he fights to stay alive for. I've never seen him kiss my mother once or even hold her.

Dead animals seem to come to my father and many days he will spend the time after supper burying them where the wolves and coyotes can't find them. Once his big black mare came up lame and he had to kill her and for a few hours after he sat beside her cooling form staring into the horse's death feeling the wind moan its way through his small barn.

In the evening, mother reads the Bible or sews things. Her hands are most comfortable with a soft patch of cloth. I watch her as I do my homework or I look out a window to where my father is working. I can not see or hear my father's tears as he enters my mother's bed at night can not feel his hand explore beneath the blanket for the places still warm for him. Neither of them went to school. They were raised on the land and stayed on it. My mother came from such a large family that she merely drifted off one day and no one seemed to notice. My father, an orphan, was

44

raised by a neighbour family fitting in the small places where they left room for him. For both of them what the body does is the most important. Words fill empty space but do little to keep the house warm.

They sent me to school to find in words a place for their story. My first day of school my mother bundled me up so much that my father said. "For Christ sake Claire give the boy room to breathe." I waited for a long time for the bus and I knew that she had been right since the cold could only make it through a layer or two of what I had on. At school, I learn that the world outside this farm is no different than here.

My mother always makes me sweaters and jackets knitting them long into the night after I am asleep. I wear them proudly even though the kids at school laugh. I can smell her next to me can see how love is passed from one to another. I remember the drought years when my father would look each day for a sign of clouds. Each night he would bury another animal. Death surrounded us. Once a lame deer limped into our yard and my father had to shoot him since its leg was beyond repair. He could have butchered it but didn't, burying it behind the house with all the others. He stood over the fresh covered earth leaning on his shovel as if he had just fulfilled some wish of his. I do not want to think about my father or mother lying in the ground waiting for the earth to be tossed over them for good. Death is not to be practiced or owned merely claimed when it is time. My mother read to me from the Bible when I was younger and the words on her lips seemed to take on a life of their own. God is something she continues to cling to even at night when my father reaches under the covers for her and she doesn't answer. This house is small and yet I have never heard any noise from their room at night as if everything intimate between them has no sound. I listen to the quiet that comes from their room sifting through it for anything of them and only near morning when the light begins to form in the east can I close my eyes and sleep.

Poseidon

Horses. He likes to keep them. Loads of them. Not to ride just to watch them spring from the corral out to the pasture. I like to rub their noses at night one after the other as if his love could be passed from them to me. Sometimes I would like to be one of those horses to feel his hand on my forehead to feel what his love is. He has no particular training in horses no great knowledge of breeds he just likes to stand among them in the corral to call one of their names and to feel her break out from the herd and gallop to him.

When I was younger, he would take me out to see them and try to get me to feed them from my hand but I was too frightened. It must have hurt him then though he has never said. When one of the horses dies he is grief-stricken for days sulking about the place. Sometimes I think he would have preferred it if I had been a horse and had come to this world not from my mother but from one of his mares. Not that he didn't love my mother it is just that he was less awkward with them than he was with me. They could sense or intuit his love and responded to it where I had to be shown and he couldn't, not without calling forth more of himself than he could.

Each morning he runs to the barn before I am even up taking each precious beast out into the field one at a time. Talking with them laughing and joking in ways he can't with me. When I get up, I watch him out the window wondering what possesses him, what drives him away from me. A father's love is difficult to find. It's not some object in a room you can hold up to the light so that it can reveal what it is you need. It is not in how he enters a room or goes to the sink to get some water. My father can sense I am watching him as he drinks or looks out the kitchen window at the pasture. But he never turns back to nod or smile.

His body is a heat I follow around the house but never find. If he enters my room at night he brings with him the scent of horses and his hands carry their caresses to my side. His hands have never held flowers or stroked my face except when I have been ill.

Among his horses out in the corral he looks not like a god but like a sad frail creature with only two legs. Sometimes I feel as though I was my father's soul carrying him forward past his death. Sometimes I hate those horses and would like to kill each one. But I would kill him in the process his small soul leaping from his artwork of bones into the flesh of someone younger.

Father's bones break a little each day. He moves as gracefully as someone dying can. The horses are my father's life each one carrying a small corner of it to a different part of the pasture. From the air they look like a random scatter of domestic creatures. But from the ground they form a patchwork that I can recognize right away. They form the stories he still remembers and believes. They help him feel that his body is not who he is.

The horses play a strange part in our lives. Their gods hard for us to see at night as they huddle together in the barn. When my father appears each morning, he is not the god they expect but another crazier creature who with his hands tries to siphon out their souls. They don't see the same world that he does. Mostly they feel safe and eat what he brings them. Their place in the world measured not by his love but by how far their legs can carry them.

Once a horse broke a leg and my father had to shoot her. All morning he paced the house looking out the window at the barn

48

as if it contained the end of his life. I never went with him but waited in the house for the sound of the rifle. It pierced the air like a scream from my father's throat. All the rest of the day and late into the night he didn't come back from the barn. Long after I was in bed I finally heard the screen door open and his sadness enter like the sigh of a dying creature.

The next day in the barn there was not a single sign of that horse or her fate. Her stall already clean and occupied by another horse. I went out into the yard into the fields to try to find a sign of what my father had done with her. But I never found a thing.

Most nights I don't see my father when I dream, although there is always the sound of horses and I never know if it is from my dream or from outside somewhere. Their sound is like a soft wind that brings its cool breath into a hot room. I never speak to them or ask them to speak to me in the dreams. They are just there faint creatures in the background living as their bodies inspire them.

Once when I slept a horse came and rubbed its nose on my window. Later I heard my father coaxing it back to the barn from where it had escaped. I never knew which one it was nor did I ever ask my father but I would look out into the herd and wonder which one had come to me and what it must have wanted to say. And I would listen at night for its return but it never came again and I knew in my heart that it had mistaken my room for his.

Looking At Horses

Horse

A horse pulled your weight as if it felt nothing behind it. Sitting in your sled you must have wondered how you felt to that horse but you never asked it never looked in its direction once. That horse is dead now and you ride in my new car as if it were a hearse. I want to ask you about riding behind a horse about the new weights that your body takes on. Instead you stop me with your eyes or with a shaking hand point out the window at some mountain I have never noticed before, thinking as I do most of the time about the weight of things. Even this car has a weight it pushes down the highway without purpose or meaning merely remaining sensitive to my foot on the accelerator.

I have never owned a horse or paid much attention to them when I have passed them grazing in fields west of the city. Always looking at the mountains instead or the city in the rear view mirror. I often wonder if you spoke to the horse or brushed its mane at night while the same stars I see shone over your shoulder. When it ate its oats did it think of you already sleeping in your warm bed? Did it care how you were driven mad by this world it knew so little about? Did it stand all night by your bedroom window fitting in nicely between your breaths?

When I think of animals I think of cats not horses and how little I know about them, accept them around me like inapt life forms. They are dangerous just like horses but I do not notice instead I feed them at the same time every day and let them crawl into my lap while I watch TV. But they are dangerous because they know already what I plan to do and they don't care.

As we near Banff I ask you about the smell of horses and you laugh and say nothing practising the silence you will use when dead. Desperately I want to be able to mystify your horse with my weight but that is not possible. Here in the mountains suddenly you have too much power and you don't want to get out of the car but would rather watch, be the tourist through tightly closed windows. Although it is nearly fifty years since that horse died you are lost without its scent ahead of you without its occasional glance back at you.

On the drive back you ask me to pull over and you get out of the car in the middle of the mountains and just listen in a way that horse must have shown you a long time ago. When I listen I hear my own heart beat or a distant car approaching. But that is not what you stopped to hear. For you there is an orchestra in the distance playing an anguish and joy that I can see in your eyes but not hear. I see that the whole time I was thinking about the horse I was thinking about weight and how it would measure me by my weight. But to the horse I would be nothing more than a faint breath behind it something that occasionally pulls on the bit. But that has no power at all. Just something that has wonderful hands and uses them to pick flowers from the earth and holds them up gingerly as if they possess a knowledge that he can never have. The horse would have known that when I fell asleep I would be dreaming of flowers and not of him. It would not have waited by my window, it would have moved as far from the house as the fence would allow.

After a while you get back into the car shutting the door as if it is something you hated. I move the car back onto the highway looking for the right space between cars. You place your hands on the dash as if they are ugly things that you want to discard. It starts to rain as we near the city and for the first time all day I notice that there is a sky above me. I stop the car for the first red light of the city and for a moment I expect you to open the door and bound off. Instead you speak for the first time in an hour saying: "That wasn't my horse, you know. It was your uncle's but he wouldn't go near your uncle he hated the way he smelled I guess. One day your uncle shot him and left him to rot out in the field. I never went out there until next spring when there was nothing left except a few bones. Your uncle used to laugh all the time about how suddenly that horse fell without a sound just boom and down he went and your uncle was smiling when he turned back to the house humming a song his mother used to sing. The air empty even before it left his mouth. He didn't need the horse anyway he had a car by then didn't want to bother looking after him anymore I guess.

"Before your uncle died he spoke to me about that horse and how he would avoid your uncle whenever he came near as if he knew, for Christ sake, what your uncle had planned for him. That horse always stayed out in the field until long after your uncle had gone to bed. Some nights I would hear it scraping its nose against my bedroom window snorting once in a while like it was trying to tell me something. Its ears turning back and forth listening for the sound of footsteps."

After I park the car and we go inside I want to go over to you, my father, and hold you. Instead I think about my smell and what it might make you feel, your mouth full of cold beer. We sit in the dark for a while drinking our beers and then you go up to bed listening all night, I'm sure, for something at your window. For a long time I just sit here waiting for the wind to die down. As I finally go upstairs to bed I feel my own weight for the first time.

Robert Hilles

Learning to Cry

Your son has big eyes and expects to be surprised every day and is. He is nearly four and the world has a certain texture it won't later. It is important for him to ask now even if the answers he gets will never be the same again. He runs to where you are sitting and he is drunk on being alive the house made up of rooms that have every mystery he could want. His skin is bruised by tripping over something but he doesn't care intoxicated by everything life gives him. You reach out to take your son's hand and he gives his so easily you know he will give up anything if you ask. He wrestles free from your hand and runs downstairs squealing with delight. You try to overtake him and find in his path a way to gain that intoxication too. But nothing works and you sit down on the floor and feel for the first time your true weight and your soul reveals itself inside you for the first time and you feel it there so carefully hidden and with your eyes you thank your son even though he won't notice. Outside birds have come to your yard and you listen as if this was the first time you have ever heard them. And their sounds are so perfect and so foreign they fill you in ways your son has been trying to show you and you bend your head and weep. Your son in another room can sense this and he waits patiently while you finish, his own eyes filling with each of your tears.

Making Enemies

I take our son's temperature while you watch. In my arms he weighs more and I have to shift him now and then to stay comfortable. When the thermometer beeps he grabs for it before I can. He laughs as he tries to keep it away from me and at eighteen months he already understands how a father can be frustrated. Finally I wrestle it from him and find the setting has been erased and I have to start over. I look down at his small face as I keep the thermometer pinned beneath his arm. I want to ask him things to find the strength he thinks I have. You come over to sit beside us and I think of the three of us as a car running outside in the middle of winter. We warm ourselves although what warms us also wears us down. Finally the temperature is taken and I release him and he runs around the house so fast his little legs are nearly a blur and you take my hand then and we both watch him and this room continues to form new mysteries for us. It, like everything else, does not set us free but holds us together and we can pretend for a little while as we watch our son running that the glory and happiness is all there is. But we know the pain will return that what we forget most is the pain but it is still there overlapping everything and a part of everything so that even a small child, like our son, soon learns that by himself and you and I can do nothing but stand over him and hope. His presence in our lives is so great now that we wake with him inside us and he gives us words to fill our mouths with and he lifts our arms and heads and for a short while we don't know what to do until we realize that he means us no harm. Later I take him up for his nap and he smiles at me as I place him in his crib. I don't speak to him I just smile back and then slowly close his door hoping he doesn't cry although he probably will. As I creep back downstairs I catch you at the window not looking out just collecting the light

and for awhile I can't go near you can't disturb what you have
found while alone.

Survivors

The wind was old that day reaching inside each of us turning our thoughts against us. Making the sea into something we could not recognize. I held my baby as if his life was all I had left. I wanted him to breathe for as long as there were days. I wanted him to see something besides death. To know when your body breaks open there is someone to save you. He cried most of the day and I hated the sea and everything on it. I watched every hour for land but it never came. I knew his life depended on land and finding it before darkness found us. But it never came. Just as his life never came. Something else came for him. I held him even in death telling stories from this life hoping he could take them with him. He was so cold and his eyes wanted to take me with him but I could not go. I tried to stay awake all night to protect his death from the others but somewhere near dawn I fell asleep and when I awoke he was gone. I looked into each of their eyes daring them to tell me what they did with him. But none would answer. Instead they just looked away into the faces of their own children. I wanted to jump over the side to find him, to lead him gently to his resting place. Something stopped me. Perhaps it was those other cold eyes around me. By the hour, we lose our humanity and what we gain in its place frightens me. It is not a darkness but it comes from inside not from the sea but inside. I know now if we survive we will take it with us on to the land. We will teach it to our children. Will alter history with it as well as our own lives. It will reach out from us and join to those around us. Our souls will no longer be seen in our eyes it will be replaced by that thing.

My son never learned his name. His body held a truth only the young have. Even when I am old I will protect his name. Say it to myself remembering his death as if it was the only thing in my life. He had no future and no past, came to this earth only to lose it again so quickly. Some think the very young have no pain, for that is something that must be learned from those we love. What took my son showed no mercy did not listen to my prayers did not give him a chance to answer back to make a plea. It was hard to free him from my body for this. But I had to.

Now the sea seems calmer and I know that soon we will sight land. Everyone on the boat is restless looking in desperation for land. Some sing, some wail, but most are silent speaking only to themselves. They have passed beyond. Some will tell stories of this later when it has all let them go. Someone may even confess how they took my dead son and dropped him over the side. Perhaps they will feel right robbing others of the disease that took him. Perhaps they will know later what a mother feels when stripped of her child. Did they say the words I would have said or did they merely look away as his still form slipped so calmly beneath the sea. Each of us knows so little we have to pretend most of the time. I no longer want to praise God. Instead I want to turn my prayers into a knife to cut her throat. I would like to hold God inside a life like mine to make her feel the agony. So that she knows that the agony takes away everything. The suffering gains us nothing despite what priests or others might claim. Perhaps we learn to hold our bitterness longer or to feed it to our children in spoonfuls like soup. I want my son back. I want the sea to have to pay and for God to pay too. But I carry on like this waiting for land.

Being a survivor is not something to boast about or make a claim to. As I step back onto land now looking at those who have come to greet us, I wonder what do they know of our lives or what we bring to them? What do they care for those who are not here? Their eyes smile as if it is to them that we have come.

Near Morning

Perhaps some of us will fall in love with them or take their kindness to be love, but I will not be one of those. I want to scream the name of my son until everyone in this crowd can never get it out of their heads. But I can't. My voice blocked by something the sea won't let go of in me. I follow the crowd into the center of the village carrying in my arms the few pieces left of my son's clothing. They no longer smell of him but only of the sea and those others huddled around me. I wish to fall to the ground to tear at it until all I have left are tears but I don't. Instead I follow the others uncertain where we are going.

I think back on all of this now from so many years later. Trying to argue with myself and with God. Trying to find words that can breathe something into my story other than what words allow. I don't wish to draw you in to convince you of the value or worth of another's suffering. I merely want you to know about my son, that his life was not something the sea could value. All lives are taken — some sooner than others. But lives taken can't be changed or gain new value with history or hindsight. They merely remain the little episodes they were. I am old now and am telling you this story so that the agony may have some purpose. However, I have little certainty that it will. I will become quiet again, going back to my life. When you pass me on the street you will not know me. Even God has lost touch after all these years. I still speak to her at night even though I know she no longer listens, if she ever did. That is fine with me. I don't pretend that I will find my son again when I die. It is not to him that I speak not to you but to myself. I wish to let out the air to leave behind these words so that the survivors will remember for awhile what has not survived. Continue to sleep as you have always done. Later you will be on your own looking for me and I will be gone.

Robert Hilles

In Praise of Children

I was old when my father was born. He entered the house one day and was there smiling at my mother as if her face was the whole world. He was just back from the war carrying it inside him for good. It was his friend. But he took my mother in his arms and I could feel them forgetting things that had passed. I was six looking for a world that was not this prairie. I was clever telling stories to my mother that she believed. Stories about my father how he was brave in his own ways. We are the oldest things. Children. We are what the future wants. My father held his sergeant's cap in his hand while he embraced my mother. After a minute it slipped from his hand and I ran to it wanting it to be my father, wanting it to prove to myself what his fingers already knew. He took the war out of his mouth describing it for us how it tasted what parts of it grew inside him. He told stories of others who were brave as if war could make someone better. I forgot his words even as he spoke them but never his eyes or his lips. I wonder even now how it is that we can kiss and kill that both words begin with the same sounds but lead to such different ends.

Each day we must become what those in power think we are like. My father never questioned the war then, only later when he was much older. Drinking in the bars when mother was dying. Telling me how much he loved her but he couldn't spend another hour by her side watching her die. The war made him old made him lose things. Things I never knew he had until I was much older and could ask him about them. He knows the terror of living much better than I do. He once hid in a farm house in France for days waiting for the Germans certain he would die soon. They never found him and even now he's not sure why. He has never told me about the few days he waited to die. What he thought. What do you think of when you are certain the end is near?

62

Near Morning

That day my father came home from the war he had to learn again where his body belonged. My mother watched him walking up the gravel road to the house. Her face pressed against the glass to hide her tears. Did she feel him inside then yearn to know again what his warmth next to her was like? Neither thought about fate but responded to the world in simple pure ways. Becoming more than the bodies that held their heat. While he walked up the road I hide behind my mother feeling her tears fill me too. When he was close enough, she opened the door and waved. He waved back and it was all so slow as if it would take forever for him to reach us. I remember how his one shoulder drooped under the weight of his bag and how he walked flatly with little bounce in his steps. I did not know then about the dead he'd seen or how he'd become more filled with death than life. The words he used after his return were the same as before but they sounded different in his mouth as if they carried a weight no word should need to.

When I was fifteen, one day he told me a little about the war. How boring and frightening it was at the same time. How you thought of silly things most of the time. How you also thought a lot about love. How you made friends easily never certain if this person would be the last to see you alive. You told stories about home and believed them. Just as you believed the commanding officers though most had no reason to tell the truth. How you drank and had sex because life was not something you wanted to lose at least not here not this way. It was hard to sleep at night never certain that more life was inevitable. He trembled as he spoke — the horror leaving him with each breath.

There is never enough room for our lives. We must fit them into such small places. Near the end my mother had little space to move in. After she died, my father hardly left the house. He shrunk back into his thoughts back to where the war was still going on. He found there the voices he needed to carry with him into death. My own son at three is trying so hard to learn to use the potty and still it eludes him like so many things do each person. He fights with me every chance he gets. The pain is old as old as all of us and still the killing continues. This week a six-year-old is murdered in Edmonton while hundreds are bombed in Bosnia.

By the time my father died he had forgotten most of the war. But what had remained was so deep nothing he did could help him reach it. I sat by his bed for hours while he breathed his strange intimate breaths. We each learn the wrong lessons making choices everyday that change the world. Still we look for instructions but get none except the bad advice of those in charge. Some of us are carried into war by the things around us. For others it is a choice our bodies make and not our minds. For the rest it is the voice of war we think we hear inside. But we are wrong. War has no voice only the sounds of the dead. But that day my father returned he was bringing us news of something hideous. It was everywhere. In his eyes, on his clothes, on his hands. He carried it into the house to my mother and me. It was not him that came home but someone the war made. I cried most of that night when in bed and wasn't sure why until years later. I could hear my parents making love next door even though I wasn't sure what it was. Once my mother cried out perhaps it was because then she finally felt what it was he had brought home to us. I never got to ask her. Now I wait in the dark for them to come back to me to tell me what it is that lies ahead. But I know that will not happen and if it did it would probably cause more trouble than good. But I speak to them any way asking them over and over again what it is that they need where they are.

Near Morning

The room is dark except where they lay. He kisses her slowly starting at her mouth and moving to every part of her body she offers him. What he discovers is how her pleasure is a new room to explore each time, where the furniture is old but unfamiliar where he has to learn to say her name with his throat first and then his tongue, where everything gives off its own music forming a chaos at once beautiful and complete. Inside each room is another room larger with more furniture and rooms inside it. He is looking for something, going into each successive room until he finds a room with a view of a calm sea and the sun clinging to the horizon. From this window he can tell her things, simple things like the colour of the shirt he is wearing or how it feels inside her so soft and not wanting to move just be inside her, fingers drawing circles on her breasts, or how from this window there is nothing that is not part of her body or that she does not have a claim on. For hours he speaks stopping only to find some new corner of pleasure for her. From her, he learns to shape his tongue and how to place a finger without harming. After many hours he opens his eyes to the few minutes that has passed and she speaks to his body making him lighter and lighter until she can lift him above her and let him float there never giving him quite enough weight to come back down. She sings a single note leaving it in her throat for hours. And the air tastes of him and she turns his tastes into sounds he can wear on any part of his body. Sometimes she bites, sometimes sucks and each gives off a sensation that makes him want to be swallowed. She learns his pleasure comes in layers that it is closer to the sounds he makes than to what she does. She discovers how he must say a name until he wears through it to a new name, must force his body outward rather than in. But he follows her even though she has no idea where she wants to go. They both know things together that they can not know when apart. True things that come from a body released of itself using fluids to express itself and reach to the dark core of creation. There in that place they find no faces, no words, no images, no light only each other trading back murmurs. Once there they hear footsteps leading them back to their room and the dark there now filling with the scents and echoes they have created and all night the fireplace burns without any wood as if fed by something their lovemaking gives off.

Near morning the moon goes away and in the dark they let their bodies draw apart. Neither enters sleep or dreams afraid what they have learned can not be taken there. In a few hours, their youngest will wake and one of them will have to go to her. Neither has a plan yet resting their bodies feeling for awhile what it is like to be without aches. The city has already started to wake up. To the west the mountains have filled themselves with the sounds of lovemaking and wait to capture the sun on their snowy peaks. Downstairs the children cross landscapes neither parent has seen and all night long search for bodies they don't have yet.

Swan

He stops the car on an old road he has never been on before. She rolls down a window to hear the frogs singing in their sleep. He crosses to her side of the car and she puts her head out the window and the night feels cool. Her hand on his pants can feel his firm bulge. She starts to tell him a story while she moves her hand over and over that one spot. Her story is hypnotic. It is about a woman who loves a swan and each day she goes to the shore and reaches out her hand. The swan swims to her and pecks at her hand first and then rubs his beak across the soft skin on the back of her hand. She is filled with a warmth that grows with each stroke. Soon she rests her legs in the water and then her thighs and the swan parts her legs enters her. She feels as though she were floating away with him. When she wakes up she finds herself alone on a strange shore her legs and thighs dry her hands still trembling in the dark. As she tells him this she slowly moves her hand inside his pants feeling his hardness. When he is spent she pulls her damp hand out and dangles it out the window. He looks into her eyes and sees that she is thinking of the swan. Slowly he shifts his hand to her panties and waits her signal. They sit like that for a long time hearing nothing but the frogs and something in the distance that could be the singing of a swan.

The Man Inside Her

He passes her window and she does not see him, thinking instead about another man. One who is inside her even when he is not here with her. Sitting on her bed she can hear someone approach and the door opens but she still does not look up. He speaks her name stretching it out longer and longer until it becomes one long moan. She places a kiss on his forehead and he falls on the bed as if spent. Then she walks to the mirror and places one of her hands on a breast and rotates it slowly as if she were playing it. He watches caressing himself too. They make music by touching themselves. Moaning and trembling feeling everything in the room being sucked into them. He crawls to her and moves his mouth to her licking softly as if he were opening the door to heaven. She rides his mouth slowly her hands moving his head forward and back. The other man is inside her still although the one who is here cannot feel him. He moves his mouth to her mouth and he tastes salty to her. His mouth is warm and tender. She weighs him with her lips pronouncing in her head not his name but the sound he makes as he crosses a room to her. She swallows him just as he swallowed her and they remain before the mirror half standing half kneeling. Each heavy in new ways. Neither looks to the mirror nor to the window but each composes the room again with their eyes closed. After awhile, she slowly moves to the bed she made only hours ago and crawls back beneath the covers. He stays in front of the mirror a long time as if listening for someone to pass outside. Then he gets dressed. He can hear her faint breath from the door as he lingers there a brief moment before leaving. One side of his body begins to twitch. As he stands there, he unconsciously moistens his upper lip with his tongue and smiles. When he leaves, she thinks of the other man still inside her his voice sounding more distant and cold. She turns over to one side and closes her eyes. She does hear him as he passes her window again. The stars remain invisible all night behind clouds.

Quick Light

There is a light in the distance, not a strong light, but one that draws them to it because it offers more than their lives. He points to it and she nods not certain of what stars mean anymore. He is not a tall man but one who stands out in a crowd because of the way he carries himself. He never lets on when he is afraid just bites his lip in a subtle, anxious way. He kisses her neck tenderly and she moves her small hand across his cheek making certain to hold him gently. She is not afraid of tears even though she has found them at the wrong times in her life. There are no tears today. Nothing but the two of them in the dark wondering how to get on. Across the city, mountains linger, faintly visible as hints of another world. Their shapes make her want to remember other nights not like this one. Cold nights when her arms, slightly numb, seem to leave her body and do things on their own. Not with this man but another, smaller man, who had shifty eyes and a voice that betrayed the words he planned to use but didn't. He told her more with his hands, than with his mouth. His life was a mess. Before he met her the sky had stars and now, look, nothing. She wanted to argue that with him but knew it wasn't a good idea and instead she smiled in the way she reserved for those she didn't want to suspect. She cared for him but was not convinced that he could see that instead he was certain that she had other ideas. Perhaps she did, she tells herself, able to admit things now she couldn't then. That other man never saw her body but saw something else when he looked at her. Not something more beautiful or less for that matter. Just a different woman who could be cruel, who could betray him in just a look out the window. She tries to recall his face and can only in a fixed expression of anger, his eyes knowing another world from this one. He made her cry a lot and on that night when they found a sky much like this one she cried not because of what he said but because of how easily he could make her hate him. Her fingers feel numb as she kisses this new man. This Tim with blue eyes that can see a faint light and imagine a sun there perhaps a whole world near it like this one. Tim can name the stars, make up stories about them. They may be true or made up and she won't care. She trusts him to lie only to make her happy. Does he trust her she wonders and senses that he might, her lies bigger though, and easier to miss. It's the small lies that usually catch you not the elaborate ones so complex they ought to be true. That other man, she can't say his name, she never lied to him the idea never occurred to her and yet he trusted her less checking each story for a slip up. He wanted lies so badly that he tried to make things lies, tried to color everything with the doubt he was so in need to hold on to. Finally in the end she began to lie to him to make him happy and she got used to it wondered what had stopped her before and she became so fond of it she found it hard to stop. Tim doesn't mind, though, he's more concerned with what gets remembered than what actually happened. He tells her that it doesn't matter what people did it is only what they say they did or how they describe it embellishing here or there that gets remembered. And if there is a god at all he or she is used to that and doesn't mind so much because what happened and even what is remembered isn't important. What is important is how we carry ourselves forward. How we maintain ourselves. How we love not because of truth or what happens but because, we can feel something inside something that can't be described anyway and can only be remembered by not describing it but by closing our eyes and holding it there again as we once did before reaching out and touching everything about it. She's not sure she believes him. Tim is prone to exaggeration. It keeps him balanced. She doesn't mind either because she likes to embellish too. It's not the stars that she likes

71

to embellish though but events in her life and all the people she meets. The ones she can barely remember, not like that other man nameless but hardly with a face now, nor eyes. Someone to hate late at night when the only companions are the ones conjured up in thoughts. She can still hear how he stumbled throughout the house half drunk banging into the furniture as if everything in the house was in his way. The others though don't garner such hate but leave her life as easily as they entered, they are harder to hold onto and they move on to other lives just like hers making no one turn around in fear. Those she is thankful for and she'd like to let them know if only she could remember them or recognize them in the crowds as they fill Calgary and other cities beyond the mountains. Tim is watching a falling star now and points to it but it is gone before she can zone in on it. He laughs and kisses her full on the mouth and she answers back with a mouth empty of words then can finally speak without their confusion. Sometimes at night he likes to wake and watch her sleep feeling softly her warm back under the covers and he whispers to her things he hopes she can hear through the murkiness of her dreams. Once or twice she will moan out and toss in her sleep and he likes that licking his lips slowly. He never tells her any of this keeping it to himself. Brenda? he will call out softly and she doesn't answer and he isn't sure why but he loves her more because of that. There are many things he hasn't told her that he will never tell her. And she doesn't ask. Just as there are many things he knows that she keeps hidden. Perhaps that will protect them best. He doesn't know about that other man. The nameless one. The one who tried to take her life one night and she hid for hours in the trunk of her own car waiting for him to leave, jimmying open the lid once she heard his car speed off. She will never tell him not to protect him or deceive him but to protect herself. The moon looks uncertain in the sky tonight and below them somewhere they both can hear a boat being rowed across the small lake. She imagines that it holds two passengers although she can't make anything out and hears no voices. She imagines a woman lying on the lap of the man who rows and wonders why she would see that. She sees her lift her hand to stoke his cheek to forgive with her hand the odd way his face is shaped. He answers by kissing her fingers while maintaining the rhythm of the oars. He can smell something on her fingers as he kisses them something that makes him want to cry or sing. But he does neither holding his breath instead. She would like to tell Tim this and watch his eyes as she unraveled this. He would not ask her why she thought such a thing and would know that years later he might remember it as happening to them and it would make both of them smile. It is best not to understand things too much that is the work of Gods and best to be left to them. It is easier to hold the one you love and pass across their cheek a certain sigh you've let no one else hear. She wants to tell him this but can't that other woman's face suddenly in her mind a face that could make her cry. She waits for him to finish a cigarette and then takes his hand and they walk along the shore and with each step become different people with entirely different lives and yet becoming again these same two people after each step. The other man might be dead now. She's not sure if she wishes that. Her life would not be served by his death. Tim begins to tell her another story about the stars one he has told her before but tells again even though he knows he is repeating himself. She likes that and listens with her whole body answering by squeezing his fingers and she waits for him to put them in the story to mark their place in it just as one does a place in a book and when he does she smiles and holds on to that part remembering it for good right there and she hears god in her stretch out and reach on to that memory and as they walk the lake answers back wave after wave, very quiet small ones touching the shore softly as one does the shoulder of a sleeping lover.

The Origin of Sound

The origin of sound is far from the ear. To find it would make little sense since what's important with sound is not where it starts but what it carries with it and what is there when at last it is heard. A boy stands on a hill and watches a brush fire in the distance. His mother calls behind him as if the sound of his name was a strong enough warning. The boy hears his name and is drawn back by it away from the smoke and his father watching with burning eyes how the smoke knows things. In his mind, he calls his son's name and his son hears it and is confused by the beauty of that sound, hidden, unshaped by the air, but carried to him all the same by some other element, one that hides sound as it carries it. The fire will burn their house in a few hours and the houses of others near by. Later some will gather in the ruins of their homes and look on with disbelief. Each charred thing contained a little of their lives. The boy stays with his mother when his father makes the trip out to the house. The ground seems oddly level as the father sifts through the ash as if trying to make it form something, anything. There are tears in his eyes he's not certain he will ever be able to dry away. He stands where his son's room was and finds the metal axles remaining from his trucks. He holds one and tries to see his son playing with what only the air can shape now. He knows there will be other trucks to buy even other houses to build he can get everything back but this. He stands in all the ash as though it was a giant sea he has no way to cross. The boy listens for his father but hears nothing. Does not see him stoop over to pick up the ash. Does not feel the marrow in his bones give a little with each step as if weakened by all the heat and smoke. Does not smell the sweet rot left over from the fire. He watches his mother instead sitting alone at the table in the hotel room writing down things. He doesn't ask her what but

Robert Hilles

lets himself exist without sound for awhile playing in his head, in complete quiet. He closes his eyes and when he opens them his father is standing at the door his hands the pale gray of ash. The boy takes one hand and holds it so hard the ash is transferred to his skin too. He looks at his hand covered in ash and smiles. His father hangs up his coat and can feel the quiet too. In this room they are all a long way from home but they have brought it here with them every room crowded into this small one. The woman goes to the window and in the great distance can see the ocean. In her hand she holds a brush and she begins to pass it through her hair. The boy can see tiny sparks coming from his mother's hair and he holds his breath imagining for a little while that he was just born here in this room the light from outside so bright and unfamiliar he has to close his eyes to keep himself from being carried into all that light.

76

Room

I am sitting in this room. I can't really describe it except to say that there is a green coat hung on the wall. Outside the room there is a large clock I can hear it tick off each second. I feel as though I am hurling through space although there is no sense of motion. There are no windows in the room so I can't look out to make sure. I can hear my mother's voice coming through the walls even though she has been dead for years. She is talking to someone and occasionally she starts to sing in her opera voice. Practicing the scales. I think. I try to talk to her through the wall even though I know she can't hear me. She was not old when she died. Breast cancer. It happened so fast by the time I made it to the hospital she was already in a coma. Now and then she would cry out strange words strung together from her life carrying no meaning. "Julie" , her sister's name. "Bacon", or "Army", "Frozen", "Fog", "Green arm", "Nails", "Accordion" words like that. And I caught each one and searched for its meaning. Trying to think of all our conversations together. But most I forgot. Her eyes were closed and sunken in her skull.

I held her hand and once in a while her fingers would twitch and I would look up wondering if she was trying to communicate through them. I would go down the hall to the lounge now and then for a cigarette and I would listen to the nurses talking in low voices. Talking about all those people dying and I listened for the details. Nearly every day someone on the cancer ward died. "314 died last night. No one was there. I had to close his mouth. His daughter called early this morning and I had to tell her. She took it well. God I hate this place most of the time." She flipped open a chart and then looked up at me over the clipboard as though I was a stranger and not the man who came each day to sit at his mother's side. I could tell she wanted to place me to know me as someone she could reach out to, care for at least for a little while. Then she looked down at the board again and went on as if by listening I was giving her permission to be truthful. "318 needs her urine bag changed do you want me to do it. Oh, I forgot the people in 304 want to take her out for a walk today and I promised to make arrangements." I could see her teeth from where I sat. Her round eyes narrowed on the pages she read as if there was nothing but blood growing there.

When she died my mother opened her mouth to speak but all that came out was a final moan. A loud low moan. A sound I had never heard before and I looked up from my book and I saw her breathing had stopped. Life disappeared from her face so quickly. But it took minutes for me to get used to the death there growing slowly minute by minute claiming each tissue I had loved and not loved. I breathed in and took a little of her death inside me and held it there waiting for a sound, any sound, to let me know she had reached the other side. I heard nothing but the room changing before me becoming again a hospital room not the place where my dying mother was. Her hands still felt warm but they were more rigid and I put my head down on her chest and wept.

When I left that room in the hospital, I left the city and my life too. I flew back to Calgary and hid for days in a room not unlike this one. I did nothing but look at the ceiling or try to see in my head my mother and I playing baseball behind our old house when I was thirteen and all that summer we did that. I can feel that summer now. Nearly taste it. See my mother running the bases while my brother walks back with the ball. There were only four of us. I can hear the wind the way it covered the trees around us and then the grass. A soft wind carrying voices sometimes and sometimes promises. Promises I could see in the trees and grass moving as if dancing, as if controlled forever from afar. When I'd close my eyes that summer I could still sense the wind coming as if for one of us from over the hills into the gully where our house sat. I would try to pray to God saying the name as if it held the antidote for everything. With my eyes tightly closed I would wait out the night climbing deeper and deeper into sleep as if in it somewhere was a future I could climb down to when I woke. But all that summer we played baseball and I never saw that my mother's red hair was beginning to turn brown. Her hazel eyes would look at me across the dinner table and I would look down into my plate as if there was a map there I could follow.

My father never came home that summer or any summer after that. He was crushed the winter before by a load of pulp wood that broke its chain and sprung over him before he had a chance to jump clear. By summer my mother was starting to smile again. At thirty-eight she was still very attractive, her face not yet bearing the wrinkles she would later need. Some mornings I would sit out in the warm July sun and listen to the birds and the occasional car on the highway and think of my father walking up the road after work carrying his lunch box as if it contained something precious. He would whistle or hum as he neared the house and I would spring out from behind an old car to frighten him and he would act really startled even though I am sure he expected it. He looked old to me much older than my mother even though he was only a couple of years older. Perhaps he could feel his death approaching and could do nothing to stop it. The day he died he spoke to my mother about going to the Lakehead in the summer for a holiday. I remember still my last words to him the night before. I was in bed and he came in to see me and standing above me he looked brave as if there was nothing one should fear. He stood there for a long while and then knelt down and took my hand and stroked it for a second and then kissed my cheek and I said. "Dad are you ever afraid?" And he said back, "Every day, and that's what keeps me going." Then he left my life for good a hanky draped out of his right back pocket and whistling a tune he'd heard long ago.

My mother carried a picture of him in a locket around her neck all the rest of her life. I had to claim it from the hospital the day they took her down to the morgue. I looked at both their pictures in that locket closed together for good now. I had to stop myself from throwing it away. I still keep it on me. It's in my right pocket at the moment.

My mother has stopped talking in the other room now; the clock has gotten louder. The odd time, I can hear a scream or a familiar voice in conversation with an unfamiliar voice. Now and then I think about the green coat. About putting it on and looking in the mirror. I always look good in green. But it's not cold enough for a coat. The coat was my father's. He should have been wearing it the day he died but it looked warm that day and he took a lighter coat instead. My mother saved it for my brother and me when we got older. My brother never wanted it so I got it by default even though I wanted it all along. Sometimes I think if he had been wearing it that day he might have seen the logs and jumped out of the way in time. Perhaps then my mother wouldn't have had to work so hard all those years to support us and perhaps she wouldn't have been too stressed to fight off the cancer. Perhaps I would have gone to law school as I had planned when I was young. Perhaps my brother wouldn't have been killed in a fight outside the Lake of The Woods hotel when he was seventeen. Perhaps my father and mother would be with me in this room and not the green coat and the locket.

The clock outside this room keeps ticking but no hours or minutes are marked only seconds. Sometimes I count them in my head counting off minutes but I never make it to hours growing tired of that after awhile. My father was always interested in time. He liked to talk to me about it at night sitting in chair drinking beer. I wondered what his friends would think of him if they could see him then talking about time as if it was as natural a thing to talk about as fishing or hunting. Time for him was male just as it is for me. Something to cross, to name, to unfold as if the stories it shaped were easy to recognize and apprehend. He liked to sit in the dark and talk about the beginning of the universe and how it grew from a single speck of light moving farther and farther away reaching for whatever was out there claiming more and more of it each day. In the dark all I could see were his eye lids open and closing even in the faint light. My mother and brother would be asleep already. Perhaps dreaming our words into their sleep somehow our faces reaching for them from some distant point in space. I never said much, mostly listened as he would talk on and on. I always wondered where he got these ideas since he never read much. Must have thought of them all day at work. Looking into the sky now and then to see if anything was revealed. For years after he died I would sit in the dark by myself and play back those conversations in my head. But I never got any further with the ideas than he had gone. It was as though he had taken them with him.

My mother would visit his grave every Sunday. It was the one day when they spent the most time together so perhaps she missed him most then. Sometimes I would go with her and stand beside her as she spoke to him. Her voice so different then and I felt as if I was listening to their most intimate conversations. She was always the quiet one and he the talkative one and now she had to carry both sides of the conversation and she found it hard. Only once when I was with her did she break into tears. She was talking to him in the ordinary way that she did. Telling him the things that had happened that week. Then she remembered that it had been his birthday and she had forgotten until the day had passed. And she was sad and told him that we would never forget it again and she didn't. That day I had to hold her arm as we walked her legs were very weak. I felt awkward at fifteen walking down the streets of Kenora holding my mother's arm. I wanted to hide but she wouldn't let me.

My mother is knocking on the door now and wants to be let in but I can't. I try to turn the knob but nothing happens and she pounds and I pound on the door but nothing happens. Does she know it's me on the other side? Sometimes I can feel her scratching on the door with her fingernails. She always kept them so short it took me by surprise at first. I ask her questions through the door but she never answers. I call my father but he is never there perhaps dead too long.

My brother always had such sad eyes. It was as though he always knew that he would die young. He had a bad temper and he and I would get in such terrible fights every day, especially in the summer. He was bigger than me even though he was younger. His red hair was so different from my dirty blond hair and I would pull his so hard sometimes that it would come out in great gobs in my hand. As brothers usually do, we fought over the wrong things. It was territorial and had little to do with love or of learning about love or coming to love clean even though all of it was love. It had mostly to do with things neither of us would want later anyway. Like my father he never comes to my door either. Only my mother singing for hours at a time.

It's hard to know when to sleep. I just let my body tire and then I slip into my dreams like a swimmer into a cold lake. My dreams are strange places full of memories that never happened of people I've never met making comments on my life or giving advice as if I was in the need of such help. Sometimes before I fall asleep I can remember very vividly my mother putting me to bed. I can only remember father doing it once, the night before he died. I remember him covering me with an old blanket rolling it back from my face. I looked up at him and wondered if he closed his eyes at night.

I tried for a long time to bring them back. Nothing worked. But I never expected this either. To be left here without rules and yet unable to progress at all. This room can't be described because you are already in it. I am facing you and see in your eyes that there is still doubt there. I watch you put a hand up to your forehead or close your fingers around a glass. I was like you once. I could see both forward and backward in time. But not anymore. I can only see behind me now. I try to find that small speck of light that my father always talked about. I try to hear his words to say them to you with my own mouth but I can't. I envy how you use your blindness so well. I am locked now in this room. Locked with you and still I can't begin to tell you yet what I know. My mother is at the door again and I put my ear to it to try and make out her words: "Bacon", "Army", "Frozen." Join me now in saying them perhaps she will hear me then.

Cause and Effect

He looks out the window and sees a bear in the alley. Not just an ordinary bear but a giant grizzly. Moving through the garbage in a graceful sure manner looking up now and then to listen and sniff the wind. It is hard for him not to ascribe to the bear various personalities and features he has himself or wishes to have. He can't hear the bear through the window and certainly can't smell it, yet he can imagine a whole life for it, the places where it grew up learning from its mother the feel of danger and how to look across the landscape for something that appears not to be there but is. In winter it learned to sleep, its dreams holding the world carefully in place. Crawling from that long sleep it crossed a stream and tore a salmon from its watery life showing in that too a grace that can't be measured by eyes or a longing for the wild.

But how did such a creature get here in this back alley surrounded by apartments? Its hunger visible even from his third storey window. He wants to call it by name to believe it would answer, would look up to him and know that someone other than god is watching. But the windows here do not open nor does a name come to him to use. He wants to know more about the bear. Its size and weight. Learn its fascinations. Its longings. The cause and effect that has brought it here into his life posing questions he wishes could not be answered. He has to leave and yet he can't must know every thing about this bear, all the places she has been and why she has now come to him rummaging through his garbage as if he'd left something for her there.

The bear has found something in the garbage that she likes and is tearing through the paper to get to it. As he watches he begins to love the way the bear knows her food not through taste but through smell and how the claws reach. He remembers when he was a boy and the woman in the house next to his shot a bear with a BB gun. With one shot right in the eye. A lucky shot his father said and he remembered thinking that luck had little to do with it. But now he is sure his father was right and he imagines a BB gun in his hand and aiming the barrel at the window remembering again it can't open protecting him from bears he laughs. The danger was real for the woman all alone in the bush her husband gone. There is no danger now. He isn't even sure if the bear is really there. Perhaps he will wake up any minute and find that it is still dark out and no bear in sight. Bears have never ventured this far into Calgary before but that doesn't make this bear any less real as her head bobs and she waves a rotting steak in her mouth.

If only he could open the window and call out determine once and for all that the bear is real. There are cars parked on the street that he recognizes and off in the distance the Calgary Tower and all these things belong to his world and yet the bear lingers as if drawn to this place as if she knew that he was waiting for her. He tells her nothing waiting at the window hearing now and then church bells or an airplane and still the bear waits finding new things in the garbage. He knows that the bear will never leave that he called her here to prove his life, to prove what she hears is not his life but the animal in him wanting to be let out. That he would come to her in his new costume of fur to offer her a human love expressed with his new body. But he never leaves his apartment. He stays long into the night afraid to turn off the light and go to bed, fears that in the morning there will be nothing but a mess of garbage in the street waiting for someone to clean it up.

Darkening

He sits at his desk in the dark looking out on a darkening Calgary. Trees outside form shapes dreams know better. He can hear sounds that night carries here for him. The sounds from a thousand different dreams fly across the night to him as he watches the few signs of traffic out the window. Night is the perfect hiding place. Each sound could be the single thing anyone of them needs to be rescued but he knows he can't do a thing, can't save any one his own salvation lost out there somewhere in the dark. He'd like to live his life backwards taking back every choice he'd made living towards his birth not his death. But would it be any different? What waits at the end is interchangeable shaped by nothing the mind knows. Still he'd like to see his parents come back to him from the grave wandering into his house leaving the front door wide open. He can see his mother's dress moving softly in the breeze as her voice comes from outside the house rather than inside it. Her hazel eyes struggle with the light as though it was something new. She sits in a chair and lifts a cigarette to her mouth which startles him but he smiles. It was his father who always smoked but now he wears white gloves and pours himself some scotch while he hums something from Mozart, he always hated music. There is so much he wants to ask his parents. But who are these strangers who know his house who seem to be able to exist without speaking, who take their time with everything?

He has tried to tell their stories. Tries to be exact. But he feels wrong in everything. He was trained as an engineer taught to imagine in other ways. He looks from them to the page and starts to whistle not sure why. Then he coughs and his mother looks up and smiles. He wants to tell her about the first time he remembers her smile but stops and looks out the window instead. He wants to hold the darkness to understand how it feeds the city and everything beyond it. It can't take him to them, can't make their bodies reunite. But he can sense them out there groping with what only death offers. As a boy he would watch his father sleep on the couch on a Saturday afternoon and imagine him floating in his sleep out the door across the streeet, to the city limits and into the foothills not stopping until he reaches the mountains in the west. He would close his own eyes trying to hold his father at the edge of some mountain dangling there so close to the ground yet completely in the air his sleep rescuing him from whatever terror he could imagine.

It is sometimes easy to pretend we don't need those we should be closest to. It was like that with his parents. For a long time he had his career and friends and that was what he needed. But he needs them now and the texture they had woven in their lives the bittersweet lives they clung to as long as they could. But now all he has of them is the few parts he can still put together. They form nothing but what memory can fashion from its dim cauldron. It consists of things their body made no sense of that he followed behind them to collect and did the best he could. Scraps really. All the rest leaving with the air, the light leaving as the night fills in each day covering so completely what has taken place in the light. There is a record all right but it never reveals what the lives actually contained, it is empty filled with words and pictures the feelings lost, just guessed at like so many things. Truth never the thing that gets recorded. He can't go back to their empty apartment to claim what little things they left behind. Things that in themselves tell of very different lives from what was. If what was can even be described or left behind for others to pick a meaning from the best they can.

Robert Hilles

Cleaning Out the Medicine Cabinet

It's hard to clean up after the dead. He looks at the old furniture in his parent's apartment. Sees his mother and father perched on each speaking to one another. Not the years that they were dying together but the years both were well and they exchanged ideas so freely. Each careful to disagree without inflicting harm. In the kitchen the sky seems out of place as it takes up more of the window than he is accustomed to. He runs some water and holds his hand under the tap for a moment. Water can numb the pain. It is the accidents that make us who we are not the plans. The plans prepare us for accidents that's all. He would like to believe in God, believe that his parents are safe somewhere perhaps even watching him at this moment. But he knows that they are hidden in something so dark that no light could ever reach it. He takes out a towel and dries his hand and the towel looks so worn he imagines that its wear held the secrets of their lives. His mother first then his father a few years after. It has been months since his father's death yet this is the first time he has been able to enter the apartment. Went on paying the rent not wanting to lose the few things left of them. They will not seem right in his basement. Piled box by box labeled to remind him for good that this is all he can keep of them. Even the memories have started to vanish. He tries so hard to replay them to give them a fresh coat of paint. But he can't. His father reading books while he begs him to come out and play ball. His mother kissing his cheek as she puts him to bed. Just as she did for so many years. His father in the living room reading looks up from his book as Clara emerges from Eric's room. "Every thing all set." He can say those words even watch them come out of his father's mouth but it's not the same. After Clara would nod Charles would go in and kiss Eric too a different kind of kiss shorter but softer as if he no longer wanted to hold things back but had to.

88

Near Morning

He can see patterns in the carpet where his parents walked. From the big chair to the bathroom. How many trips a day did his father have to make near the end, his kidneys so weak? And the ones to his mother's room where she made her way slowly into death. The pictures on the wall remaining the same as the day they moved in. He remembers his mother hanging each one telling him about some of them. He looks now at the picture of his mother at twenty-one and he can't imagine what she was like then. He knows that inside her somewhere he is already starting to grow. Her eyes uneven the picture capturing that in a way he never noticed in the flesh. He finds it strange how photographs transform us. What did people do in all those years before photographs more comfortable with paintings seeing what the artists sees. The artist able to lie in ways the camera can't and yet it does because this isn't his mother either. It is merely what the camera could find in all that light.

His father is better looking in his pictures than he was in the flesh. The camera able to hide certain flaws in his face. A picture of his father at thirty-five shows him how skinny he was then. God people were so much skinnier in the 1950s. Used to eating less and working hard. In his right hand his father is holding a camera and he can remember seeing it sit on their dresser for years. It's gone now lost in one of their final moves and lost with it is the truth these pictures need. He has no idea how he can ever take these pictures down. Thinks instead of keeping this apartment for years coming now and then to see.

He finds one of his father's books left open on the coffee table. He picks it up expecting to find a message from his father but there is nothing. The book will not close and he examines it more closely hoping that it will contain his father's secrets. But it is just one of the books his father never finished. He holds it a little while expecting it to tell him the meaning of his father's life. It contains mostly poems and he feels awkward approaching them knowing that there are easier ways to lie.

Eric sits down and reads each poem and then tries to close the book but finds that it resists closing. The poems seem buried in their own words and he tries so hard to find what they are. But like his father they are fixed now by the moment of writing down just as his mother and father are fixed by their deaths. He sees that saving someone from death serves no purpose just as these poems serve no purpose until they are read. They make no sense to him and that makes him sad because they should. He remembers the poem his mother use to like reading to him Tiger, Tiger burning bright but he can't remember who it is by. Tries to piece it together in his head watches his mother's mouth as he hears her recite it. But he can't hold on and his mother slips away as do the words.

He goes back into the kitchen halted by the sight of the spice rack hanging on the side of the cupboards. The spices are in alphabetical order and he can watch his mother as she arranges them. His father used the spices but was never keen on keeping them organized. When he would come over for supper he would watch one of them reaching up for a spice or two, the reaching hand guided by the other's eyes. He has no idea if his parents were really in love though they acted like he thought people in love should act. What secrets they held they took to the grave with them leaving nothing behind to instruct him.

Eric decides to start in the bathroom. He carries an empty box he has brought with him. Opening the medicine cabinet he is surprised by the number of medications there. When he would visit sometimes he would snoop through it to see what they were keeping from him. Usually he found nothing. But today he realizes that there was a great deal of pain they had to live with. He shuffles them all in the box not able to bring himself to read the labels like he once might have done. His hands feel cruel as they disturb the order his parents had established over the years. The box is full now of pill bottles that seem to carry no weight at all. They were the only protection his parents had from death and yet they believed.

He has to stop himself. Carrying the box out into the living room he sits down and cries. The tears seem to come from every part of his being each tear filled by a different ache. In crying he can feel his parents leave the various parts of his body he has stored them in for years. He cries and shivers at the same time. His body suddenly consumed. Eric has become all that they have left behind. The only living evidence of them and he knows that and doesn't know that. His spine curves allowing him to bend into his grief with a new shape. The sunlight through a living room window warms him slightly as he lays in the form his grief has given him. He doesn't move for a long time but learns to hold this new posture for good. When he does stand he is completely transformed completely shed of them. He tries out his new arms and legs shaking each one briefly. He looks around him and is pleased. They will remain here forever where he has left them. At the front door, he looks back once before closing it. He smiles then knowing he will be back and next time when he comes he will be alone.

Robert Hilles

You Can Carry the Wind — Rilke

And so you must, moving it from place to place as if its shape and meaning were learned from the bodies that carried it. The wind travels through the world claimed by the motion of planets and space not by what poets find easy to put in poems. Down some sidestreet a faint wind makes its way past some children huddled there in safety. One of the small children will take the wind into her mouth and dance to it, the movements of her dance looking grotesque to anyone who might pass at that moment. The child will spit out the wind and laugh knowing for the first time what the wind is careful to let go of. The wind will move on not guided by animal behaviour but uncertain of what it means to be swallowed by a child, especially one willing to let it go. The rich think they can carry the wind in their pockets tossing out small bits of it now and then like a coin thrown to the poor. Some look for evidence of wind, others have lost faith in proof altogether since it leads to such sad consequences. Most wander the streets trying best to avoid the wind, their lives already too full of things to explain or fear. However when the wind becomes a menace, when a severe storm is near, each will take cover as best they can fleeing the path of the wind, all the while knowing that in this, as in all things, the wind appears random turning at the last minute to save a house, perhaps even a lone child hiding beneath it while moving into the path of another claiming all lives. Each of us tries to hold the wind inside with each breath carrying it for a little while as if taking it home to shelter or kill. We can watch those others stagger as the wind fills parts of them they don't expect. After awhile they will have to let go and the wind will travel through the streets like a freed animal never once looking back. The wind will stop for awhile when some distant force changes its whim and for a moment the rest of us relax knowing

Near Morning

we can't reach the wind now or where it is going its time inside
us not enough to show us how.

Robert Hilles

What Language Can't Reach — Rilke

The boy closes his eyes and sees a herd of horses and he knows that nothing prevents him from opening his eyes and seeing the horses there but he keeps his eyes tightly closed counting the horses and giving them names as he notes each one. He could reach out with his hand and stroke the head of one or two, but doesn't. In the middle of the herd there is a white horse with a few spots of black on his nose and this horse draws him to her with the promise all animals can make. He begins to speak to her saying her name almost as a whisper. Parts of him begin to sway and dance and a great song lifts up from the horse's mouth not a human song. The boy opens his eyes suddenly and must close them again the light is so bright. When he opens them a second time he expects to be trampled by the herd led by the white horse. Instead there is nothing but this heat and a grass so still as if mesmerized by the heat. He lifts his hands to shield his eyes and spans the horizon for any sign of movement. He imagines god like this place hot and still moving forward but watching all the same. He is a young boy and has just begun to learn the value of a god. It is less important to him if god has eyes or a face or a gender. He would prefer a place he could walk to and talk to himself all the way but remain quiet. And that he could swing himself on to the back of a horse and leave cities, nations, arguments, and anger behind. He could ride alongside his father and mother and they would be laughing.

His own father sits by the house a few blocks away and wonders where his son is. He has forgotten to look in the field where his son is even though he went there all the time as a boy. He has even forgotten god mostly except perhaps late at night when he wakes as himself.

Near Morning

He calls his son's name a few times and then heads off in the opposite direction from the field where his son sits. The boy can feel his father moving in the world but can't place exactly where he is. Each thinks of his body as a place where the world starts but are confused by the presence of others, especially creatures such as horses who have learned through the generations to be still and yet possess a speed and grace people can only marvel at. Their eyes are so big and on the sides of their heads needing them to be shielded at times from things they might otherwise fear. The father can remember other horses though, temperamental horses easily spooked that would flee suddenly no longer held by the fence. Hours later he would have to round them up calling quietly their names coaxing them with a voice he could use for his son but hasn't. The boy has never ridden a horse finds them hard to approach even at the Stampede each summer. Still he dreams of them mounts them for hours searching perhaps for where his father is lying down. He can't get the white horse out of his mind nor its name as he slowly makes his way home. He knows his father will ask a lot of questions but none of them will be the right ones and he will answer as if he didn't know what he wanted his father to ask and both will be thinking of horses but neither will communicate that. The boy will go to his room and begin to draw pictures and it will be of men upon horses shooting other men and for him that will be beautiful and for some reason he will not feel the pain of those men whose bodies he has drawn on the ground nor imagine for those a name that can be recorded. But the horses and the riders will have names and places to go home to and perhaps boys like himself who imagine war first but not the pain. His father will sit downstairs reading the paper passing over most of what is there because it contains pain. He will not read about the children killed in Bosnia nor of the woman's body found west of the city. He will turn to the sports page and look at pictures of men and women who have learned to disbelieve their own body pain. Some will be captured in the awkward stance of exertion. They will be looking over their right shoulders as if towards home but all that will be there is the dark eye of the camera. He will not put down the paper for a long time but will hold it long after he has finished with it. This is how the world comes to be more of what it is. The quiet things have no chance of being heard. The father can't remember being a boy anymore and what it means to imagine soldiers lining up to die. He wanders through his work and life, drawn more by the places his son wants to go than anything else. Once there, he is usually uncomfortable and looks at the other mothers and fathers around him, and most are the same watching their children grow towards the plans they keep in their heads. When he puts down his paper, the boy will be asleep with his face pressed into his pictures on his desk. The dreams he follows for the first little while he is asleep, seem to take place in the same field he was in today, but now it isn't horses he sees when he closes his eyes, but his own father reaching out a hand coaxing him back.

Quiet Nights

for my father
Austin Edwin Hilles
(1920-1995)

I miss his quiet.

Wintertime

My brother phones to say my father has been drunk every day since he got back from Calgary a month ago. Once he got so drunk he shit his bed and my mother had to clean it up. At seventy-three he doesn't know where to go anymore or even what colour the sky is if it has a colour at all. Once he was a bird but he forgets more of the sky everyday. The air he holds in his clogged lungs is stale old air incapable of supporting flight. While he was visiting he didn't drink much but sat by the window looking out most of the time, not saying anything. I realized for the first time that he is old and most of his strength is gone. Strength he learned alone listening to the night like a love song. He didn't walk much at all taking the bus the four blocks to the grocery store. He muttered to himself and I tried to interrupt him to discourage him from doing it. In his head he holds the arithmetic of a different life than this. I can sense it in his eyes but nothing of it ever surfaces. We sat together now and then and tried to talk but all I could think to do was ask him questions. He didn't want that. Didn't want anything to do with questions there'd been enough to feed a hundred lifetimes in his life and what they referred to was pain and for that he preferred to close his eyes and imagine the wind.

He had a bladder infection while he was here and had to go to the bathroom every hour all night long. Once I went downstairs to see him sitting on the toilet looking so white and he looked up to me like a child unsure where he's just been or is headed. I walked up to him and put my hand on his shoulder and we stood there in the bathroom light both naked looking into the mirror as if another life was taking place there. He squeezed my hand once and lowered his head as if about to pray. I looked at the top of his head and remembered red hair where the pale brown now was. I wanted to stroke his head and sing him a song one so right that both our hearts would know it. But I couldn't. The light interfered with my thoughts. Instead I backed away leaving him there captured in his old age, a prisoner to how his body wears out. I wanted so much to see him as a boy, to imagine his face covered in peanut butter and jam to hear his higher voice filling the air with sounds the universe could not preserve.

The doctor the next day found his prostate enlarged and recommended that he receive further diagnosis in Winnipeg but my father hasn't followed through. Like most things in his life he prefers to let it be. I tell my brother perhaps that's why he's drinking. I may have scared him too much with talk of cancer and pressuring him to do something right away. Perhaps he's learned the world best not me. I open the window he looked out all the time he was here and listen to the traffic and feel the air slip in a little unsure of what it should do. I move his chair as close to the window as I can and I inhale and listen and wonder what it is we expect to see all by ourselves. I thought of the one time my father took me hunting near Longbow Lake. We sat in the bush for a long time not making a sound. That was the way he liked to hunt. Most people like to send out one person to chase the deer back to where the others wait in ambush. He'd didn't like that. He preferred to wait and then to stand up and announce himself to the deer before shooting. As we waited, my legs got so stiff and numb, I had to rub them to keep the circulation right. He never moved his body once having learned this pose a long time ago as a boy. We didn't see a deer that day. Near dusk we made our way back to his old truck. He didn't say a thing all the way back. Only when we were at home did he say, "Don't be disappointed some days are like that but it's the days like that which make you a hunter." I wasn't disappointed. I didn't like killing things and I didn't want to go back. But sitting by the window now I can finally see what he means about hunting.

As I hide in the light from the window, I know that the sky was once a place we could not go to but now it carries us from one life to another and we don't notice a thing. Right now I want him to be coming in the front door saying my name, laughing and singing sweeping the children up into big hugs but he was never like that nor am I. We started our lives in different places but ended up here in a future neither of us could see before but are left in like survivors from a ruined voyage. There is no stillness in the city not like what we found deep in the bush, a stillness that leaves you with a sense of belonging. In wintertime we'd sometimes wade through the deep snow back behind the house. He'd have snares for rabbits and now and then he'd catch one. I'd wait off at a distance while he slipped the carcass from its noose. I'd never eat the things although he'd tell me over and over they tasted fine. My mother wouldn't eat them either. Only my brother and him. Sitting in the dark kitchen finding what the moonlight means as it traced their eating for them.

From the window I try to find what he must have found to focus on as he ignored my mother not even listening to her as she spoke to the back of his head. I don't think it had anything to do with the lives of my neighbours conducted carefully around him. Perhaps he wasn't looking for something at all at least not something lost but trying to erase what is there, to make it all go away. If I close my eyes, I can see our old road still aimed out of the wilderness to the highway, a thin thread of ambition through it all. I didn't see it that way as a boy. The highway was a fearsome thing that took us away from what was safe. Perhaps my father still sees it this way having only lived in the city the past seven years. He longs for the bush less now but still claims to miss it whenever I ask.

When I was ten, my father had his index finger on his right hand cut off at work. They kept the end of his finger wrapped up in tissue as they drove the ten miles to the hospital. The cut off piece was sewed back on but it attached incorrectly and the end of his finger was bent down in a hook. Each time he visits I look at that hook again and wonder. It has made it harder for him to sign his name all these years and yet I love that about him. Imagine the pain during that ride into town the other men making jokes to keep him alert. When he points at things the hooked part is aimed wrong. I imagine him sitting in the dark at night rubbing that tip to ease away arthritic pain and through that frail landscape of pain his life drifts in and out of his head. Lost to everyone no matter how hard any may try to recover it. I want to sit with him in the dark and hold his hand to trace with careful words how his life has run out. But I can't or won't. How does he imagine my life? How does he imagine who I am? Once I was a boy who was easily led to mischief. But now? Someone ordinary with a mortgage, family and thrifty. I am careful not to repeat his mistakes but in doing so I make a new list of ones that my children will use as a guide to get away from me. Perhaps that is the most important thing. Perhaps the making of mistakes leads us into the right places after all.

Near Morning

I close the window and put the chair back to where it suits me better. The children play upstairs already living alone. I say their names in my head and the sounds they make take shapes all their own, ones not invented by my mouth. In my head I speak to my father and it's the only way I can speak to him about such things. I ask calmly, carefully: *Why did you sit so long at the window? I liked it better when I would pull up after work and see you sitting in the porch. I liked to think you were waiting for my safe return from work although you didn't act as if that's why. Only after I was inside for sometime would you wander in smiling in a way I've seen no one else do. You hadn't shaved for a week and you rubbed your face with your hands and walked to the fridge for a beer. There are things I want to ask. Things I want to describe about your life but can't each thing I depict is not your life at all but mine. I have loved you in the oddest ways but it is still love. When I am old will I understand? Do you? Right now my head contains things I never expected that it would. When I was in Oregon this summer I thought of you as we spent a day by the sea. As the waves rushed the beach with automatic precision I thought of the rough edges of the sea and of the wilderness things we file and plane down not even sure yet why. I thought of your rough hands and face and how the years of manual labour etched a dignity there I can't reproduce here. My son wandered into the water too far and I had to run in shoes and all to retrieve him before a wave claimed him. As I dragged him screaming and thrashing to the shore, I thought of you teaching me to swim in Longbow Lake and how I hollered and cried and how patiently and gently you persisted. I wish I had that patience and gentleness with my own children often I worry like crazy doing things I despise later. It's crude the way we act as parents most of the time making it up as we go our sense of direction lost in the dark somewhere. Through it all, what persists is a strange kind of love not summed up by words or actions carried deep inside us somewhere nour-ished by little things. Now and then we take time to examine it or to speak to it like we would someone of our own making. I don't admit enough things claiming a perfection in words that is not possible. I've made too many things, been too mean at times and demanded too much. I see too I have none of your grace or calm. And yet you drive me crazy with your drinking and your quiet. I wish I could show you the life I've practiced in my head. It's not the one you've seen nor has it resisted all you've taught. When I was driving away from the ocean, I followed it in my rearview mirror for as long as I could. It was like watching a faint trail of my own life make itself visible for awhile behind me. I closed my eyes for just a second as I drove and I could feel my life more precisely and I could feel how as I moved ahead I was staying perfectly still my life in motion but frozen too. It's the emotions, feelings that hold us in place no matter how right or wrong they might be. It's that I've learned from you and imagine what it is you saw all those days at the window the house so quiet with all of us at work or school. My mother wandering behind you a part of your life but held at bay for some reason I can't ask you yet. I will close my eyes now and see that window again and again a part of my house and my life and yet part of the world too a small frame of light fit in around the dark.*

Lungs   *Calgary March 22, 1994*

When my father called to say he had lung cancer, I remembered the night he came into my room when I was a boy and took my hand because I was afraid. My mother was in the mental hospital in Port Arthur then and I'd been having a dream where she was wearing a dress of flies and her eyes were a fly's eyes seeing a thousand different images of me and she didn't know which one was the real one to claim and as she chose one it would vanish into thin air replaced by another. I must have cried out because I woke suddenly to find him standing near the bed. He sat down and took my hand and never said a thing. My mother would have used words to comfort me because for her words were comforting. But not for him. Only confusion came in words. Instead he sat silently looking into my eyes and squeezed my hand. He smiled deeply and I held that smile inside me as preciously as I could, as deeply as I could. My brother slept on beside me and I felt protected by my father and all the quiet around us, a quiet that contained the whole damn world, and perhaps none of it at all.

I put down the receiver, my father's voice lost inside it for good. I looked out at my backyard and I could see him standing there building the playhouse for my daughter. He was caught by something in the sky and just stared at it for a long time, not even noticing that his work had been interrupted. My father's voice was heavy inside me too and I scanned my body for its location. I wanted to hold him so much and to return back to him something he gave to me that night so long ago. But he was 900 miles away and I was left with only my thoughts realizing, for the first time, how little they contain.

2

The doctor said he's only functioning with one lung the other so full of cancer. I can't stop thinking of all those years when I was a boy and I'd watch him puff on cigarette after cigarette. The smoke he was feeding himself contained his own death and yet it made him stronger too holding in his lungs all that smoke as if it belonged there inside him, heating him. When he got drunk, he'd smoke more lighting each cigarette carefully with his zippo lighter. The kind of lighter you have to fill by soaking the bottom cotton with lighter fuel. Every Sunday he'd sit in front of the TV and fill his lighter checking the flint too. He'd hold the flame high into the air his arm extended. The flame would catch for a moment in his glasses and from across the room the flame would hide his eyes from me. He'd snuff the flame with a snap of his fingers and look at me and smile knowing that every time he did that I'd flinch. I could feel the flame on my finger tips long after he'd hidden the lighter back in his pants pocket and gone to retrieve another beer from the fridge. Now he only smokes two cigarettes a day and his breath on the phone sounds so strained the single lung doing the work of two. He is even quieter on the phone his own death a visible place on the horizon now. He talks around it but the shape is always there behind him somewhere practicing for him. I phone every day my voice too loud as it leaves my mouth as I try to compensate for his quiet. He puts the receiver down quietly as if it contained a life line he needs too. I sit for a long time with it in my hand knowing inside it my life has been sucked and waits there and only my ears can find it again. When we went fishing in my youth, a cigarette was always dangling from his mouth and when he was done with it he'd simply open his mouth and let the butt drop into the water. Soon after there'd be another in its place. Sometimes I thought it was the cigarettes in his mouth that kept him from speaking but it was something else, something the cigarettes merely signaled but played no part in. Whenever one of us caught a fish, my father would wrestle it into the boat while carefully balancing a cigarette between his lips. The dying fish would try to make sense of this new place opening and closing its mouth. My father would sometimes hold up a fish right near his face and smile the smoke from his cigarette filling the dying fish's eyes. He'd drop it then solidly to the bottom of the boat. The fish's fall broken with a thud by the wood there. As the day passed, the fish would collect in a small squirming pile. Some fish died fast others wiggled for a long time. Below us in the water we returned our lines time and time again retrieving from the water all the fish we could eat. I never liked to touch them they felt so slimy to me but I loved to watch my father wrestling free each hook from the fish's mouth. All the while he smoked his plain cigarettes and smiled at my brother and me teaching us as best he could about his world. I'd like to take the cigarette out of his mouth now and throw it into the water but I can't and instead I keep him in my head protected there as best I can.

3

My brother called today to say that the cancer is further advanced than the doctor first thought. I think now of my father's life in days, weeks perhaps months but not in years like I did just a few days ago. Nothing fits into my hands and anything I try to hold slips from them to the floor. Every July he'd take us up the hill from the Cameron place where we moved after the fire. He'd take us there to pick blueberries. Sometimes I'd grow tired and would stop to eat some but he never minded. He was gentle with me and my brother even when he was drunk the fear was mostly in me. From the berry patch we could see the house below and behind it the highway and Longbow Lake. My father was happiest here lifting the berries into his pail. His hands would be covered in blue stains when he was done picking. All of our hands looked bruised as we carried our berries back to the house. Andrew and I would wash our hands as soon as we'd reach the door but my father wouldn't. I'd catch him sniffing them and now and then licking away the blue and purple marks. We'd eat the blueberries with sugar and milk after supper sitting outside, the night air filled with the occasional sound of cars on the highway. From up on the hill the lake looked smaller but fuller, its shape more defined from above. I could see the little inlet where Andrew and I would often go swimming. Each time we climbed the hill, I'd look for the spot as soon as the lake was in full view. I'd try to make out if anyone else was swimming there and now and then there would be some people who had ventured up to this quiet end of the lake and decided on a swim, but mostly the place was empty and I liked that thinking of it waiting for us. When my father got older and Andrew and I moved away, he stopped going to pick berries. Once when I was twenty-nine, I asked him to take me again. The path up was grown over and a few times we lost our way. The berries weren't particularly plentiful. The lake looked almost exactly the same though with the addition of a few more cottages across the bay from the highway side. I looked as I had always done for our swimming spot but it was harder to find and I had to ask my father to point it out. He hesitated for a moment and then pointed to a place that wasn't it, but I never told him that.

Near Morning

4

There wasn't much sky around our place. Not like the sky I've learned to love on the prairies. In northern Ontario the trees and hills block out the sky, and mostly what you are left with is a small patch of blue directly above you. My father liked that absence of sky but I never did. I wanted more sky because in all that blue and white I could imagine my life better than I could down here on the earth. The sky had a life of its own separate and completely different from ours and what went there was changed for good by it. Old man Smith's son Kenneth fell from the sky one day when his bomber was shot down over Berlin. Others too have fallen out of the sky, offered back to the earth that made them. There are others still who enter the sky and never return slipping through a seam in all that blue and vanishing. For years my mother thought that was what happened to all of us when we died, that we float up into the sky and melt into it becoming something it hides from us. She told me a story too about one of her sisters that died really young. My mother said her body lifted up out of the bed where she lay and floated out the door up into the sky. Everyone ran out the door to follow. My grandfather tried to retrieve his lost child from the air, but he missed and so did her mother. She floated up above the trees and then vanished into the glare of the sun. No one in her family said a thing but my mother ran back to the bed where her dead sister had just been and the bedding still contained the shape of her body. The impression left there though was faint as if her body was already very light when it lay there. I thought for years that it was just another of my mother's crazy stories but now I know what she meant the sky so big where I am the miracles are much easier to see.

5

My father was sick all winter with a cough and I should have been more forceful about him going to the doctor. Although my brother had taken him several times and even once a doctor had made a house call but they didn't see. Like all of the living they didn't want to see the small marks death starts to make on each of us. Or perhaps they just saw an old man and didn't see the point of going any further. There is a lot of wind outside today and I start to hate the prairies and the mountains to the west of us and all the wind they bring. The sound of wind has always frightened me. When I was a boy the trees around our place would bend so violently with the wind that I'd expect at any moment they would snap in two. But they never did holding onto their place with a might I'd wished I had. Out here there is little to stop the wind and it rattles the house making me want to cringe as I often did as a boy. When the wind got too great during a thunderstorm I'd hide beneath the bed. My mother always thought I did that because of the thunder and lightning but it was because of the wind. A few times she got under the bed with me and we sang together until the storm passed. Andrew would calmly sit out in the kitchen enjoying every part of the storm. He'd always make fun of me when I'd emerge from the bed when my mother gave the all clear signal. His laughing would usually lead to a fight and I never hated anyone as I did him in those moments. I would begin punching at his head. All the while he'd continue to laugh until mom would break us apart. My father never laughed, though he just accepted my fear as if it was a natural thing. He never tried to coax me out of it like my mother did. After the storm I'd usually go out in the damp air and smell the things the storm had left behind. Spruce and poplar branches would be strewn all over the place and I'd try to pick some up but would tire after awhile the work too great. Instead I'd go back inside and see that everything was as it was before the storm. My father and brother watching TV and my mother in the kitchen humming to herself breathing in something the storm couldn't erase.

6

Every spring my mother would clear us all out of the house while she did spring cleaning. None of us volunteered to help. She'd wash the walls and the uneven wood floors as best she could. It would take all day and sometimes late into the night but we were never admitted back in until all the work was done. We'd saunter in, not at all careful with our progress. With our every movement we'd erase something my mother had done but we never saw that. Only she did as she watched us with a frown on her face. Spring cleaning was something her mother taught her, but at least she'd had all those children to help her. Mother never insisted and we never volunteered that's what bothers me now. My mother still spring cleans each year. Even this year with my father dying of lung cancer, she calls to say she is washing the walls. "Spring cleaning" she says a joy and purpose in her voice. She doesn't make my father leave anymore perhaps he's learned to not mess things up so quickly. He never volunteered and now he's too sick to. He watches TV while she works around the walls. She describes the dirt for me later over the phone. Then the house was all her own for a few hours and I think she liked that the best. The three of us pacing around outside not sure what to do. On those days my father and brother never touched the old cars. Just waited outside with me even though we all knew it would take her hours. We paced like expectant fathers used to waiting until once more mom would let us in.

7

I don't know what to say to my father now that he is dying. I still call and the words fit in our mouths as they have always done but once offered over the phone line they fade until all they carry is their sounds and nothing else, all reference lost. I ask my father about his childhood to fill the space between us. I count the days until our visit hoping that something I've said or asked will make a difference although I'm not sure it will. My father is brief answering each thing I ask him with fewer and fewer words as if they too were leaving him once they were used. I try to cheer him up so that he will fight the cancer better and I remember him doing the same to me when he tried to teach me to swim. And the time I cut my leg with the scythe and he had to drive me into town for stitches. Later he was upset because I called the doctor a liar when he said he was done because I was expecting more pain than that. He made me apologize to the doctor although he never made me do such a thing before or since. I didn't feel I needed too but I did anyway because he thought it was important. When I was burned in the fire, I walked up and down the hospital corridor screaming in pain and he talked to me calmly trying to settle me down. My brother who was burned too merely whimpered now and then but didn't say much. My father's words were a salve to me and I quieted because something in his voice took the pain away. What I offer across the electrical maze of the phone lines isn't enough and he leaves the phone early every time, something he hasn't done in years. Mother always rescues the phone from his hand waking me with her manic words and offers his good-byes for him her mouth too close to the speaker.

112

Near Morning

8

I learned in school that an isosceles triangle has two equal sides. And the things that men build rely on such rules to make them work. I watched my father for years wrestle with his cars. I'd watch from the kitchen window as his dirty head would bob back and forth under the car hood. It wasn't until much later that I saw that the angle of the hood made it an isosceles triangle and each time my father put his head beneath the hood he was breaking some spell. Whatever I learned in school my father showed me that there was an alternate version outside school. For a long time I thought it was important to go to school to apply myself and become educated. Later I learned that education was different for the rich and poor in this country. Back then I thought education was the same everywhere. It wasn't until I went to the University of Western Ontario that I found out different. But my father knew all along, and as I poured over books as if words themselves were the world, he showed me with dirty hands something else. When he got too old my brother did all his mechanical work for him. He still pokes around under the hood with my brother but he mostly watches or carries on some conversation with Andrew that I wish we could have. But beneath the hood and behind the wheel my father's world was very known. It eased up from the earth itself and the magic it contained was something the earth could teach you if you listened. Now his lungs fill up and release and he is dying and his hands can't hold a wrench anymore. But they take my hand as firmly as they have ever done even though we are 900 miles apart. I trace in my mind his slow progress around his small apartment in Winnipeg. He's on the toilet sometimes when I call and my mother fills me in on things as she waits for him to be finished. When he comes on the line the phone melts in my hand and I want to walk along the wires all the way to his place retrieving along the way the words he dis-

113

cards into the line. Geometry was never my best subject and even now it baffles me. But buried in it somewhere is a ruin that is valuable to rebuild. We pay attention to our lives and act as if certain rules can protect us. In geometry somewhere is my father's life and my own and I need to search through rule by rule until I find where we are. Rectangles and triangles all around us wrapping us into the strangest shapes imaginable. It's time some of it got written down.

Near Morning

Arctic Ice Company (of Winnipeg Manitoba)

I found it in storage at the Glenbow Museum. The Arctic Ice Company's Little Arctic ice box. The same kind there was on the farm near Kenora where my father spent his youth. While at the Glenbow, I discovered that the real museum was in the back, hidden in the shelves waiting for some unknown future. In all those rooms and rooms of things from around the world, it was the ice box that caught my eye. It was as if a single specimen had been collected from my father's life and kept there preserved from the sun like his remaining days. He'd told me so many stories about the ice box I had to stop and look inside, to see how it was made. Mostly by hand I could judge with only a few simple tools to help. Tin lined the place where the ice block was kept. The tin molded by hand into a crude shell with awkward corners waiting to receive the ice. I could see my father dropping the ice into place, his hands still tingling from the cold. And as he spun around, in that small hot kitchen the ice made quiet settling sounds as melting water dripped down the pipe at the back into the pan that collected it at the bottom. The ice box was so small that it could hold only a few precious things, most of the food kept in cans or eaten while fresh. I can't imagine what was stored in there. I ask my father but he can only remember carrying the ice down the hill in the hot July sun, facing the light with all his strength. The ice's cool shape holding everything in his life.

Each trip down the hill was the same. Near the house he'd hoist the ice high into the air as if to tease the sun. The cool melting water would run down his arms tickling his armpits and he'd dance a little the last few feet to the house careful to never drop it. When he tramped in with the ice Mrs. Smith always smiled lifting open the lid for him. She'd hand him a cool glass of water for his work and he'd sit quietly sipping it as the sunlight eased

115

its way through the west windows turning the dark of the kitchen into something bright and calm. When he was finished his drink, he'd hand her the glass and head outside again to other chores sucking the hot air through his chilled mouth. The sunlight was all over him carrying deep in its heat something he thought could stop time. He'd see Royal Smith out in the field somewhere working through the rows of beets or beans. My father would always wave at him but the old man seldom waved back. My father would go back to his chores feeling the cool line on his neck where the ice had rested all the way down the hill as it dug deeper into his neck the sun in the west still high enough to make his forehead sweat. And as all that sweat and ice water drained down his body, he became the meeting place of hot and cold. Still he'd work his way down the hill stepping over tree stumps and ant hills, the tall grass beating against his legs in time to the cool breeze, his mind feeding on all of this saving as much as he could so he could offer it up to me later when he was dying, the words slipping from him like shallow, empty breaths and I'd take it all in believing every word, every sound of it because in all of that the world gets known for a little while.

The Arctic Ice Company of Winnipeg made ice box after ice box by hand throughout the 1920s, starting with the wooden frame and then the metal shield around the wood to protect it from rot and then that long pipe straight down the back. The Arctic Ice Company sold them to farms, cottages, and homes some lasting into the 1950s, left in cottages to cool beer and pop in the summer. Such a simple plain design, little engineering involved just a wood frame to hold a block of ice to keep the things beneath it cool on all those hot summer days. The Arctic Ice Company. My father didn't remember the name. I found it again for him in the Glenbow Museum. Each ice box made in Winnipeg and carried by train to Kenora before the highway was open. The Arctic Ice

Near Morning

Company. The perfect name. I was looking for a miracle when it was the name that mattered. The ice just kept things cold. It was the name that made the ice come back again so my father could hold it one more time in his hands the glow from the ice melting over his skin bringing a smile to his worn lips.

My Father's Dreams

My father told me that since he's had cancer, he has been dreaming his life over again. People and events exactly as they were once lived. He tells me that with a curious smile like a child on the first day of school. He has never told me about his dreams before and that strikes me now as strange as if only as he approaches death do his dreams take on a significance worth sharing. I wonder too if I'm in those dreams though he never says the details.

My hand closes around his, and the light from outside covers the table at my brother's camp the same way it did ours at home when I was a boy, and my father's face would always be lost just a little from that light as if he wanted a part of himself, always hidden, his life draining out without the least bit of a record. I could never tell then if he was ever smiling or if what the light could not reach was a sadness that he wanted kept secret. The light always made perfect sense to me while the dark was something you crossed to more light. Today his face is completely revealed, the light slipping across it shows how the years have marked their way on his features. He is smiling as if he hears something beautiful from his life the dream from the night before pointing his way although he won't share it with me. My mother listens but can't fashion my father from any of the words he admits to, claiming instead from the light a whole different person.

I get up from the table and trace around the room the evidence the light has put there of his dreams or even of our lives wound together by something our bodies can't find. There is pain in this room and suffering not thought out by a God or made significant by any great historical event. Instead his dreams remain locked in

118

his sleep racing through his mind with a heat and clutter that can't be siphoned out by anything I do or ask. He looks good for someone with cancer and I forget as I pour a glass of water the sound of his breathing so struggled as if he was climbing a steep hill all night.

I was nearly born in a taxi he tells me one night and he smiles as if he's found the right seam at last taking my hand as he usually doesn't do and smoothes away the grains the years have worn in place. I can see him in the taxi his mind going blank for a moment as my mother twisted with the undulations of birth. He must have turned to the driver in earnest then, though he doesn't say. My mother puking into his lap as if her insides had turned against her. I wonder too if that ride comes back to him his spine curving against his past with all its strength. If there were a God now would be the time for it to prove itself crawling across the spaces in my father's mind making room for the things he needs the most. His life, nearly finished behind him, has shape only in the things it carries like a willow tree hidden beneath a layer of spring snow. Trees and wind know things a God ought to and my father in his old body knows things too that matter the most when he dreams them, the events of his life stored carefully in his brain the wind crossing it too a large expanse measured only by the size we can put into place by our thinking. He tires easily his eyes drooping as he rides beside me on the way back to Winnipeg. The city grows before us containing so many lives like ours I ache from it. I turn to where my father naps his head against the car window and try to find evidence of his dreams on his face but everything is hidden by the light. I see that what the dark left there is easier to see that my father was right to keep part of his face hidden from the light because he left something for me to find now as he crosses again some event from his life. Whether I am in that event or not doesn't matter for it's what the dark has left there for me so clear on his face his life not what is found by the light at all but something else as slippery and pure as any life can be. The car drones away the last parts of my father's dream and my hands on the wheel feel so cold I want him to reach over and warm them with his breath.His life he holds onto the best he can and I love that about him. The car continues to carry us away from where we should be just as time does. Never able to go back except in dreams near the end of our lives putting together something that has no shape except in the fragile forms of memory and what is left there when we are done no one else can make sense of, the wind blowing the last few ashes away and we stand back in awe because who could ever imagine or behold that a life could be this.

My father sleeps on as I ease the car into the parking stall of his apartment and suddenly his eyes flash open and I catch a glimpse of a young boy in them as he sorts out what place in his life he is at and what place in it he has just left behind in his sleep.

Aero Bars

I visit my father in the hospital while he is getting chemotherapy, and I bring him three Aero bars. I am reminded of the time when I was burnt in the fire and he would visit me every night bringing an Aero bar, placing it on the table for me and I would always wait until he said good bye and was gone down the corridor before I would open it and take a bite. He would never prod me to eat it while he was there, understanding in some unexplainable way. Today, as I sat in the hospital looking out over the green park across the street, the IV dripped into my father, and I could see him when I was a boy, the sun shining on a Saturday morning, him standing with one foot on the fender of his 51 Ford half ton, the sunlight bringing his face fully alive. He didn't say much, just smiled and chuckled to himself and then would get in the truck and drive away. He laughed today as I told him a joke. The teenager in the next bed had his appendix out and the phone kept ringing for him, never a call for my father, just for that young man. My father sat so patiently in the hospital, letting the IV pour into him, believing with all his life that this, if nothing else, could save him. My mother and I took the elevator back down to the street and we embraced, neither shedding tears, as we supported one another. Knees trembling a little as the elevator touched ground. We didn't say much as we crossed the parking lot and I tried to find his window again to wave up but the declining sunlight filled each one and I could see nothing but an uncomfortable glare dancing off those shimmering pieces of glass and my mother and I bumped against each other as we walked towards the car. It waited there like a dead thing, doors creaking open as we each selected our appropriate side, one slamming the door after the other and I backed the car away from its parking spot as if I could leave certain portions of my life behind and cut away from it and head somewhere else. As I drove I could see my father's face in the windshield caught there by some trick of light and dark. I could trace his every feature, watch his eyes as they took in the horizon, not filled by it alone for each thing has an appropriate place in his life as he lays patiently on the bed, hardly making a sound. Most of what he has done has been accomplished in silence, his eyes, seeking me, sometimes fixing on me in a way that could make me uncomfortable or happy, depending on how I looked away. As we were driving on the highway a few days earlier, I was rubbing my father's back and I was reminded of when I was a teenager and we'd sit, I in his arms watching TV and I realized that I'd forgotten the tenderness we shared all those years, instead, I built up an amazing fabric of lies. He fooled me too. I was afraid even as I grew older. I see his eyes are tired as he laughs at my silly jokes, and tries hard to show me that he loved me and it was me that backed away all those years, it was me who took away the things he wanted and discarded and left behind everything else it was me that didn't say I love you. As I stood beside my father, laughing on the Cancer Ward, I was taken in by those blue eyes and I wanted to touch each one to find with my fingers a slight hint of what they saw, instead, I lifted a hand to his cheek and stroked it. He smiled a little, his gaze drawn away from the IV drip for a little while. He looked almost happy, except what drained into him was now a complete mystery, his life being filled with things he wasn't really expecting and I turned away once more, backing out to the door embracing only for a moment then backing downstairs.

Later I stood at the mirror, balancing my hat awkwardly on my head. I moved it first to my left side and then to my right side, just as I saw my father doing a few hours earlier when I had offered him one of my hats and as I watched something in me was set free. At the mirror I saw that I was trying so hard to be my father, to be the things not that he had taught me but things I have noticed as he passed me in the house, the things I'd seen those few days when I was alone in the hospital and he would come with the Aero bar and it's not because I praise it that I want to be that, but because in all of that, in all of the learning, the studying, the unraveling of his life into my life, and my life into my children's and their lives into other lives, in all that massive unraveling, something got put back into place, something we didn't even notice until turning back we could see it there, glistening, just as it ought to be in full view, showing us the way we'd come

My Father Is Dying

My father greets everyone we meet in Kenora, when they ask *How are you doing?* with *I'm dying.* Each person takes the declaration in a different way but most stand back for a second to breathe in something they hadn't expected and then slip down a little as if their guard was dropped without their willing. He then proceeds to tell them about his cancer. I admire that straightforwardness, something that he has always had and I want to grab him in my arms at that moment and say *It's not yet, it doesn't have to be this way.* But he goes forward into his death, straight forward into it, acknowledging it, with each person he meets. I'm not saddened by that but a certain joy enters me that I don't expect at this age, the joy that carries with it the knowledge that my father has proved himself as best he can and what he is doing now is continuing with his own grace, moving towards his death inch by inch, head up, acknowledging it, knowing that fear does no good here or anger or pain, just straight up with your eyes wide open, embracing it, like the deepest dark of any night knowing inside somewhere that what vanishes is not yourself but what you were afraid to let go of before but can now and your son trails behind you, his eyes wide open too but still afraid of everything he sees, his fingers taking hold of something, perhaps his own life, perhaps not, then as he trails behind you, he lets out a word now and then, almost in praise but more like a question. He can't ask himself nor you but falls behind you, making notes, putting words clandestinely on the page as if in their frail fabric of sense they could match even a small bit of what you are able to accomplish in that single sentence *I'm dying,* not as a plea, not as a question, as a simple statement, *I'm dying, don't be afraid, don't back away, that's simply what's happening. I'm dying. I don't want you to feel sorry for me, I don't want you to be sad, I just want you to know that that's what's happening to me.* And I think of my father at fifteen, covered with leaches the summer he dove into the slough behind old man Smith's farm to clear the beaver dam and when he came out his skin was covered with a fur of them and one after one Mrs. Smith picked them off like one might fruit from a wonderful tree and tossed them back into the water, returning things offered by a God who is willing to take his gifts back and then she cradled him as his flesh quivered from all the marks they left behind and they walked slowly up to the house, old man Smith sitting on the front steps laughing a little bit, not making fun, just laughing because this goddamn life is so funny sometimes. My father standing there with those dark things glistening on him and he was whole for a while, whole because he refused what little flesh they might have wanted and his body shook a little as she plucked each one carefully from their dangerous pose and he was in love with the world then, just as he is now when he says *I'm dying.* You have to say that sometimes. To stand up in the church or in the movie theatre and announce it, *I am dying,* but that is not why we come to these places, these houses, equipped with an odd assortment of furniture displaying in their own intimate way the anguish we all share. I remember stopping at George Smith's to find for the first time photographs of my father hidden for years in boxes, almost discarded but suddenly giving a new life to him as I saw him for the first time how he looked as a boy, holding that goddamn rake, his hands filled with the work he was about to do and the work he had finished so carefully. His life eased around him like a warm wonderful thing and he was alive and I could see it in his eyes in those pictures, oh God, he was alive as he was again when he looked briefly at himself across the delicate framework of time staring intently at those grains of history. I could see how wonderful life can be in those moments when the deepest things are found and we look around at those we love and know that they can see it too. The pictures glistened in that warm sunlight and showed me how my father once stood there so proudly, his eyes filling with the light. In one picture he is nearly eighteen sitting by a rock and he looks so much like my brother with his knees pressed into his chest, I am a small part of that body then just as I am a small part of this now and I cry for every moment as it happens and he is alive and yet he is so purposefully saying, *I'm dying, don't look at me any different, just know this, capture it, take it to some place where I will never go and open it and drop it carefully before you, like you might a single precious element you have been able to latch on to and as it falls there and something grows from it, that is at once perfect and yet so flawed it will easily erode its way into oblivion, just like all of us have done,* and still he comes into the brightest day of the year, stands before someone he hasn't seen in twenty years and says so matter-of-factly without warning *"I am dying", let's get on with it, for Christ's sake, I am dying, don't cry, don't ask me to cry because dying is what all of us will do one by one some haphazardly, some by accident, some by intent, we all will do it not because we want to or need to, because like every day that returns not by magic but through some pattern that we make sense out of or try to shape before us and realize that what we are doing is undoing patterns, slipping carefully into chaos. Let the dying be, just like the living are, careful, step by step, negotiated, obvious, matter of fact, graceful, nurtured, wistful, beautiful, magnanimous, exact, imprecise, whimsical, illogical, stirring— all of that and yet more than any word or group of words or masses of words could be or utter or explain is not what is observed at all but transfused by a flesh to form some logical, simple act of profusion, careful without pain with its own logic that spreads before the day not with any predefined pattern, but like a drop of water on the sand vanishing so quickly that nothing is tangible except what transpires in that briefest of moments so faint, it wouldn't show up on a pane of glass and yet it happens all at once right there within anyone's grasp.* When my father greets you and says *I am dying*, don't stand back, don't turn away but understand that he is giving you the one gift he has left.